DECLAN

The K9 Files, Book 21

Dale Mayer

DECLAN: THE K9 FILES, BOOK 21
Beverly Dale Mayer
Valley Publishing Ltd.

Copyright © 2023

All rights reserved. Except for use in any review, the reproduction or utilization of this work in whole or in part by any electronic, mechanical or other means, now known or hereafter invented, including xerography, photocopying and recording, or in any information storage or retrieval system, is forbidden without the written permission of the publisher.

This is a work of fiction. Names, characters, places, brands, media, and incidents are either the product of the author's imagination or are used fictitiously. Any resemblance to actual events, locales, or persons, living or dead, is entirely coincidental.

ISBN-13: 978-1-773367-53-8
Print Edition

Books in This Series

Ethan, Book 1
Pierce, Book 2
Zane, Book 3
Blaze, Book 4
Lucas, Book 5
Parker, Book 6
Carter, Book 7
Weston, Book 8
Greyson, Book 9
Rowan, Book 10
Caleb, Book 11
Kurt, Book 12
Tucker, Book 13
Harley, Book 14
Kyron, Book 15
Jenner, Book 16
Rhys, Book 17
Landon, Book 18
Harper, Book 19
Kascius, Book 20
Declan, Book 21
Bauer, Book 22
The K9 Files, Books 1–2
The K9 Files, Books 3–4
The K9 Files, Books 5–6
The K9 Files, Books 7–8
The K9 Files, Books 9–10
The K9 Files, Books 11–12

About This Book

Welcome to the all new K9 Files series reconnecting readers with the unforgettable men from SEALs of Steel in a new series of action packed, page turning romantic suspense that fans have come to expect from USA TODAY Bestselling author Dale Mayer. Pssst… you'll meet other favorite characters from SEALs of Honor and Heroes for Hire too!

Doing a wellness check on a War Dog—now in the care of a woman who trains therapy dogs—Declan sees the aftermath of an attack. The trainer hopes for some assistance in how to work with the War Dog, Shelby, but apparently someone didn't want Carly working with Shelby at all. Or was the attack connected to something else in Carly's past?

Carly has been through enough heartache for a lifetime. Her parents were murdered a few years back, leaving her alone in the world; even worse, the case was never solved, leaving her stuck in the past. She'd done her best to move on, … but this attack brings it all back.

The situation goes from bad to worse, as yet another attack involves an old friend, as he tries to explain something about her parents' case to her. It's hard for Carly to believe, but is it possible that the attacks on her connect to her parents' murders? From Declan's point of view, how can it not?

Sign up to be notified of all Dale's releases here!
https://geni.us/DaleNews

PROLOGUE

KAT LOOKED AT Badger, as he hung up the phone. "Good God. Even listening in on Speakerphone, I have to ask. What the hell was that all about?"

"One very convoluted dog story."

"Will there be charges for everybody?" she asked, looking at her husband in wonder. "It's hard to even sort out who did what because so many angles are involved."

"There will definitely be a lot of charges. I've already contacted the war department about the family who knowingly sold a War Dog into a dogfighting ring over in Scotland. They're assessing what options they have, and they've been talking to the Scottish authorities as well. I would think the family will be prevented from adopting pets, at least for a time, but they also aided and abetted a dogfighting ring, and that is a crime over there, so they aren't getting away free and clear by any means."

"I can't believe all those murders." Kat stared at her husband. "Such little regard for life."

"That is stunning and over how many years? A decade? Just amazing. Both of Kascius's parents, and nearly his brother and sister-in-law, plus Ainsley's brother too. It's a miracle there weren't several more murders."

"Kascius did say the plan evolved as needed, but, at one point, they would all be killed by Angus, so he could get the whole farm and sell it. How did he think he would get away with that?" Kat cried out.

"One of his early plans was to knock out Kascius, making it seem as if Kascius had killed Liam and the rest of them, before he killed himself—all in some angry PTSD event. But I think, in the heat of the moment, once it all came down, everyone was just reacting."

"It's all so crazy. My God. You know I'm half scared to pick the next case after this one." She sat back and looked at Badger. "Yet some of these case files are pretty compelling."

"Here I was thinking that tracking down a dog and taking it back to the family or finding another family would be all there was to it, but some of these cases end up pretty convoluted and dangerous as hell."

A cough at the doorway had Kat looking up and smiling. "Hey, Timber. How are you?"

The huge tree of a man sported a tinge of silver in his hair to match the blue-metal prosthetic on his right leg. He shrugged. "I'm fine. As always."

"Which means you're holding but not fine," Kat pointed out.

His gaze narrowed, and his lips twitched. "Blunt, aren't you?"

"To the point, you mean." She didn't back down. Timber had been in and out of the Titanium Corp office for a good six months now. He was one hell of a carpenter and a handyman, had been a hell of a Navy SEAL, and now wanted little to do with anyone. He was polite, respectful, but a loner. Some of the men here were friendly, happy to go with others for a beer, a walk, just to sit around, or enjoy a BBQ. Every time Timber was invited, he refused.

"What do you need?" Badger asked the new arrival.

Timber hesitated. "There's a few acres one mile or two from here …"

"Around Gando's Pond?"

Timber nodded. "Yeah. Any idea who owns it?"

Badger looked at Kat, who stared back at him. "You know Killerman, right?" she suggested to her husband.

Badger nodded. "Andy Killerman. He's got a place close to it. Why?"

Kat watched Timber wrestle whether to share or not. Finally he shrugged. "I was wondering if it's for sale."

"It's a great piece, if you could get it," Kat said warmly. "We have often looked at it and wondered."

Timber nodded. "I'll talk to Andy."

"Do you know him?" Kat was surprised. Timber never seemed to speak to the others. So knowing someone outside of this group here was surprising.

"No, but I will." With that, Timber walked back out.

Badger looked over at Kat. "What was that all about?"

Her laughter rang free. "I'll say he's looking to settle close by but not too close."

Surprised, Badger nodded. "He's a hell of a good guy. But that piece is what? Twenty acres? It won't come cheap."

"I think it's closer to thirty acres. Yet wooded and pastured, with a creek backing onto Gando's Pond itself. If Timber can get it, that would be a hell of a coup. But what would he do with it?"

The two looked at each other. "Does he like dogs?" Badger asked, with a grin. "Our War Dog files will dwindle down eventually, as we near the end of the requests from the war department. Yet, as we both know, there is a hell of a need out there for someone to help out these animals in other ways."

Hearing a bark, both Badger and Kat turned to look out the window. And watched as a dog raced toward Timber. He bent down to greet it, his face lighting with joy. Too soon the dog was called back by its owner. Kat turned to Badger. "Well, that answered that question."

"Yeah, but I'm not sure Timber's ready yet to be a full-time dog owner."

"No, not yet. Timber is still a mystery I've been trying to understand for months."

"You and me both. Not to mention the rest of the team is also curious about Timber."

Kat added, "But back to today's issue. What else do we have for cases?"

Badger looked down at the file he had chosen next. "I don't know what to do about this one either."

"What's the matter?" she asked.

"There's a woman doing animal therapy and training, who says she ended up with a War Dog and has no idea how she got it."

Kat frowned at him. "That's a twist."

"It is. She has provided the registration number, and it fits a War Dog that went missing."

"So, what's the problem? Case closed, right?"

"Somebody still needs to go do a welfare check on the dog, and honestly she sounded really nervous on the phone. Maybe something is deeper there than it appears on the surface."

"Nervous how?"

"I'm not sure, but I've got somebody in mind for this one. Do you remember Declan?"

She frowned at Badger. "Declan would have come work for us but then went in for more surgery or something, wasn't it?"

Her husband nodded. "Yeah, he was in a friendly fire incident that took out his leg, a couple ribs, and also broke his collarbone."

"That doesn't sound so friendly," she said in disgust.

"I know, but he lives in the same state as the animal therapist, so it seems to be a good fit for him. I was thinking about giving him a call to see if he's up for helping out a little damsel in distress."

Her eyes widened. "Do we really think this is a damsel in distress?"

Badger shrugged. "All I can tell you is that she sounded really nervous on the phone."

"Well, hell, let's do it then."

With that, Badger reached for the phone, again putting it on Speakerphone. "Declan, Badger and Kat here. So, do you want to be a hero?"

Declan laughed. "Always. What do you need?"

CHAPTER 1

DECLAN KANTOR DROVE slowly down the street in this small town near one of the many forests found in Oregon. Declan lived in Oregon too, about three hours from here, but had yet to visit this part of the state. The houses in this neighborhood had large acreages involved, so most of the homes were set back off the street a bit. In a section up ahead, the houses were a little closer to the actual road. Still, most looked to have privacy and space, which he totally approved.

He checked for the address he sought, and, even as he glanced up, he saw a young man stepping from a small Victorian style house, set about one hundred yards away from the curb. The man pulled down his hat and walked toward the street.

Declan drove past and realized he was one house too far. He pulled up on the side of the road, put his vehicle in Reverse, and quickly backed up. As he did, he watched the other man head down the street at a brisk walk. Declan got out, checked the address on the street, and realized that the man had come from the same house Declan was looking for.

Hopefully someone else was home. But then again, this was a woman who dealt with therapy dogs. So there should be animals at least. Not that they'd answer any questions. As Declan walked up through the little white picket fence gate, and headed to the front porch, he noted that the door had been left ever-so-slightly open.

He knocked on it and called out, "Hello?"

When no answer came, he swore and stared at the open door. He pushed it open a bit more and stuck his head in farther. "Hey," he called out, raising his voice. "Is anyone here?"

When he saw no sign of anyone, he stepped back out, walked down to the street, and searched for the young man, but he was gone. Declan checked the address again. Even though the address wasn't posted on the picket fence itself, there was one posted on the house.

He took out his phone and quickly called the woman who lived here, as he stood outside on her front porch now. He heard it inside, ringing steadily, so he was definitely at the right place. He frowned at that, and, just as he was about to hang up, he got a text on his phone from Badger, asking if he had arrived. Instead of answering with a text, Declan gave him a call. "I'm on the front porch of the house."

"What's the matter?"

"The door is slightly ajar, but I can't raise anybody. As I drove up the street, I watched a young man leave here, and the phone number that you gave me is ringing inside the house."

Abruptly Badger said, "Go in."

"Yeah, but I don't really have any authorization to do so."

"Remember that part about her being nervous? I'll hang up. You go in." And, with that, Declan stared down at his phone, ended the call and pocketed it, then pushed open the door. As he stepped in, he called out once more. "Anybody here?"

He saw nobody, but, in the background, he heard dogs barking. But that would be normal and expected, since this woman dealt with animals all the time. He took several more steps into the living room and called for her again. There was nothing, no noise, no response, but he was getting an odd prickling down his spine.

He quickly walked through the first floor. As he came into the kitchen, he swore and raced to the woman, who had collapsed on the floor. She was a little thing, and Declan couldn't miss the blood on her head. Immediately his ire rose, along with his protective instincts.

He bent down, checked for a pulse, and immediately pulled out his phone. As soon as he got through to emergency services, he explained what had happened, as much as he could quickly tell the operator. "I just knocked on the door, and it was slightly open, so I don't know anything much about it."

"That's fine," the dispatcher replied. "We have somebody on the way. Please stay at the scene."

As he crouched beside the woman, he immediately placed a gentle hand on her back. "It's okay," he murmured. "You'll be fine. Just take it easy. Help is on the way."

She groaned slightly, shuddered visibly in front of him, and opened her eyes—revealing her amazing forest-green irises—staring back at him.

"Are you all right?" he asked, his tone worried.

She blinked several times. "Who are you?" She glanced around and frowned. "Where am I?"

"My name is Declan Kantor. I came to talk to you about a War Dog. Your door was slightly open, and, when I got no response, I found you on the floor of your kitchen, so stay still. Whoever else lives here with you just left, but I missed him on the block. I have to admit I was a little worried, so I came inside." He winced at his audacity. "Now as I know more, that was probably a good thing." He pointed to the backyard. "I hear a lot of dogs barking."

She blinked at him owlishly and reached up a hand to her head.

He immediately grabbed her hand. "Don't touch," he murmured. "There's some bleeding, and I'm not sure how badly you're hurt."

She stared at him, then it seemed like she connected to the barking of the dogs. "Where are the dogs?" she asked, frowning.

He shook his head. "I can hear them, but I haven't gone around your house, so I can't answer that."

She groaned, closing her eyes. "They were in the back. I heard somebody in the house, or I thought I did, so I came inside without them." She muttered to herself more than anything else. "Why would I have come in without them?"

"I don't know," Declan replied. "Did somebody call you or cry out to you? I don't understand what might have happened."

"Neither do I," she whispered, her eyelids falling closed. "Oh, God. My head hurts something awful."

He winced. "I'm sorry." The color of her face was really pale, her eyes beautiful but shocky. "I can hear the ambulance coming. Just stay where you are."

Her eyes widened in horror. "No, no, no, I'm not leaving."

"Well, something's definitely wrong, and I can hardly leave you here on the floor of your kitchen," he explained, trying for a lighthearted joke. Yet it failed miserably, and she just stared at him.

"I'm going nowhere, and nobody can afford an ambulance in this county anyway," she stated, with a certain level of bitterness. He had seen that a couple times before when it came to medical assistance for people without insurance.

"I'm more concerned about you, making sure you're okay. Do you have any medical condition that would make you collapse?"

She stared at him. "Yes." He frowned at her inquisitively, hoping for more information, and she shrugged. "Okay, but I haven't collapsed in a very long time."

"What kind of condition?"

"I get blood pressure drops. Sometimes it happens for no reason."

"How long since your last attack?"

She glared at him. "You're hardly the police or a doctor," she snapped. "I don't need to be answering you."

"No, you don't. I'm just a concerned citizen."

Immediately her face flushed. "I'm sorry." She struggled to shift her position, but he immediately held her down.

"No, stay still, please. You have to at least let somebody look you over." At that, he heard a voice at the door, and he called out to them, "We're in the kitchen." That was quickly followed by two men moving toward him. Declan explained, "I found her unconscious on the floor, with an obvious head injury. I don't know whether she fell and hit her head on the way down or has been attacked."

At that, she stared at him in shock. "Attacked?"

He looked down at her. "I don't know what to say. I don't know anything about who lives with you. All I really know is that I found you on the floor."

"Right." She was still blinking, with that very disconnected look.

He stepped back at the request of the EMS team and watched as they worked on her.

She tried to shift at their behest. "See? Not bad at all," she stated.

Yet Declan watched as a wave of pain washed over her. "Maybe, but you're obviously not well."

"I'm not bad either," she protested. "I'll have a hell of a headache though. I presume I slipped on the floor or something."

"Is that a possibility, or are you sure?" one of the paramedics asked her.

"I have a lot of dogs around, so it's happened before."

He just nodded and didn't say anything.

At that, Declan looked at her and frowned. "Maybe, but the dogs are outside. So I'm not sure that's a good-enough explanation for the injury."

She stiffened and glared at him but didn't argue.

He watched the EMT proceed carefully, making sure that she was looked after properly. When she declined to go to the hospital, they confirmed that the injury looked to be something she would be safe with at home. However, they warned her about headaches and ongoing problems to watch for. They made it quite clear that she might need to go to the hospital for a proper checkup.

By the time they pulled out and left, she was sitting at the kitchen table, looking a little worse for wear. The dogs in the background kept up their cacophony.

"So, do you want me to let the dogs in or to deal with them somehow?"

"If only I could think a little bit, I could tell you, but, at the moment, that seems a little hard to do."

He just nodded and sat down beside her.

She looked over at him. "Who did you say you were again?" He pulled out the ID card he'd made before leaving on this trip and held it out for her.

"Oh, the War Dog." She sighed. "She's such a beautiful animal."

"Right, so I did need to come and check that she's okay here."

"You mean, that I'm not doing something to hurt her?" she asked in a hard tone.

"No, not at all," he replied. "Yet this isn't typically the pathway that these animals take, and we have a responsibility to look after them."

She immediately flushed. "Sorry, it's been a rough day."

"Sounds like a little more than a rough day." At a quick look around the kitchen, he spied the teakettle, so he got up and pointed. "How about I make you a cup of tea? That might help settle you a bit." She didn't say anything and just stared at him in surprise, so he quickly put on the kettle. He stayed quiet, as he puttered around to find a cup. Locating a teacup too small for his hands, he put it on the table before her and, at her instructions, put two teabags in.

When the kettle whistled, he filled her cup with hot water for her.

"You're quite competent around the house."

He smiled. "Practice makes perfect, and sometimes, whether we like it or not, we gain expertise in areas we don't particularly want knowledge of."

"Not sure what that means," she said, reaching a hand to her temple. "Man, oh man, I'll have a wild headache."

"You're already having it," he noted calmly. "Head injuries can be really dangerous."

"I still don't even know quite what happened." She

looked around her kitchen, frowning.

"Let's start with the man I saw walking out of your house."

She stared at him. "What man?"

"When I drove up the street, I was looking for your address, and I saw him walk out casually from your house and head down the block. So, as far as I can see, he was the last person who would have seen you, prior to your injury."

She blinked at him. "So it must have happened just after that then."

"Unless you can tell me who it is. Who lives here with you?"

"I don't live with anyone. The last thing I remember is that I had just fed the dogs outside, and we were going through some practice training runs, some exercises just for fun. Agility type stuff to keep them happy. Then I heard something, and I remember shutting the pens and coming inside."

"You came in because you heard something or someone inside the house? An intruder? Why come without the dogs?" he asked, one eyebrow raised.

She flushed. "I guess that sounds stupid, doesn't it? Honestly I didn't think. I just shut the pens and ran."

"Would you have let in a stranger?"

"I don't remember even …" She stopped, frowned at him. "I don't remember even getting that far."

"It's possible that you didn't. What if the intruder came in on his own?"

"You keep talking about an intruder," she said in a testy voice. "I don't have any reason to believe that."

"But neither do we have any reason to believe that the man I saw was a friend. Particularly when I came in afterward and found you on the floor."

She took a deep breath. "Can you describe him?"

"Tall and lean, like six two and brown hair. He was dressed all in black."

She swallowed and shook her head. Then shuddered in pain. "It's not ringing any bells," she murmured, "but then it might take a bit for my brain to make a connection here."

"It's possible," he noted. "I mean obviously something is still going on."

"No, it's not even that," she said, as she wrapped her arms around her chest, waiting for the tea to steep, staring at it with such a longing of comfort to her.

"I guess you don't have any coffee around, *huh*?"

"Absolutely. Would you like some?" She sighed. "I'm sorry. I'm not a very good host."

"That's fine. I don't need to be looked after."

"Good thing because it's the wrong day for that."

At her attempt at humor, he just smiled, then stood and walked toward the coffeepot. "How much coffee should I add for a couple cups?"

At her instructions, he quickly made a little coffee, and, when it was done dripping, he brought a cup over to the table. She now hugged her hot tea brew in the teacup in her hands.

"So, I don't know who the man was. I guess the only suspicious thing that told you something was wrong was the fact that he didn't shut the door, so I guess maybe I do owe him a thanks for that."

"What? For being a sloppy intruder?" She glared at him, and he shrugged. "Hey, I call it the way I see it."

"Except I don't know that he was an intruder."

"But you also don't know that he wasn't."

"Right." She groaned. "Regardless I'll have this cup of tea, and then I'll go outside to confirm the animals are okay."

He nodded. "I looked out the kitchen window. They are fine."

"Well, that's good news, and hopefully whoever was here didn't have anything on their mind."

"Outside of knocking you out?"

"Is that what it looks like?" she asked. "I was thinking I fell, or maybe I hit something. I don't know." But she reached up and checked the wound on the top of the back of her head. "It could be an assault, couldn't it?"

"Sure looks like it to me," he agreed.

"Damn, what would be the point of that? I don't have anything here for anybody to steal."

"Are you sure? Some people would steal for five bucks."

"That's just a sad world," she muttered. "Sure, I have a bit of money on me. I work hard, and I work from home. I do have a job, besides running my own business." She gazed at him incoherently, lost in her thoughts. "Still, I don't keep much money in the house."

"Maybe they didn't know that," he suggested.

"I don't know why they would. I don't know very many people here. I'm friendly enough with the neighbors and all, but it's not as if I've been here forever."

"How long have you been here?" he asked curiously.

She thought about it and replied hesitantly, "A few years. Enough to be comfortable but not enough to get to know very many people outside of my immediate sphere."

"Right. Yet long enough that people have obviously figured out that you are here and may have thought that you have something. I have to admit that this guy did not look like he was a junkie or homeless or the type to make a quick buck off something that you had—or even looking for a meal. He was dressed all in black with a ball cap on his head, which stopped me from seeing much of his face, plus I was looking for your address. I wasn't looking for an intruder."

"Right, that kind of changes the way you look at things, doesn't it?"

"It sure does," he stated.

She closed her eyes and sat, just resting.

"I think you should go lie down," he suggested.

"I have to check the animals first," she murmured.

"I'll go check on them. Tell me what I'm looking for."

She snorted. "Dogs, that's what I have. Four of them are out there."

He nodded. "I'm pretty sure I saw four, but hang on." At that, he hopped up and walked over to the kitchen window and looked out.

"Four," he confirmed. "Not a one of them looks like the War Dog though."

"No, Shelby's in another pen," she told him. "These others are all pretty well trained and mostly pets."

"So, are they pets or are they going out to work?"

"Well, both really. They do go out to work with me. I go to hospitals and to the pediatric center close by. Plus, visit a couple nuclear medicine clinics every once in a while, depending on what their caseload is like," she explained. "These are therapy dogs, so they go out and meet with people. Sometimes they can make the patients feel better and can make it easier for them to get through some of the treatments they're having. I've been training them to help reduce the patients' fears a little—especially the kids, when they need special treatments." She smiled. "Those four dogs are mine, and, depending on what I'm doing and where I'm going, some are better with certain things than others."

"Right. So where would the War Dog be?" Declan asked.

She stared at him and blinked. "She's out there."

"But in a different pen?"

"Yes, but still out back."

"I'll be right back." Then he opened the rear kitchen door and stepped out onto the deck. His gaze scanned the backyard. He poked his head back in and said, "Hate to tell you this, but no War Dog is out here."

CARLY SIMPSON STARED at the man across from her. Tall, dark, big, broad shoulders, and the tapered waist of an obviously fit male in his prime. "I don't remember what your name is," she murmured. She glanced down at her tea, then back up at him.

He smiled. "Declan. And you are Carly Simpson?"

She nodded. "Right, and you got all that information because I called in about the War Dog, correct?"

"Yes. That's why I'm here, for the War Dog."

"For the War Dog that is no longer in my backyard."

"Is there anywhere else it could be?"

She shook her head and then shuddered with pain.

"How about I take a walk around outside? You drink your tea and get your bearings, and, when I come back, I'll have a second cup of coffee." With that, he stepped out into the backyard.

As soon as he was gone, she slowly got up, made her way cautiously to the bathroom, wincing the whole way, just to check out what she could of her head. It was obviously a head wound from behind. She used the facilities and washed up, then took a wet washcloth and held it up against her head, trying to clean up as much of the blood as she could. It was sore but didn't need stitches, and she really hadn't lied to him.

She didn't remember a whole lot. She had come running into the house, pushed open the kitchen door, and, after stepping forward, there was only blackness. It wasn't hard to surmise that whoever had been making noise in her house had hit her over the head and had dropped her.

She didn't really want to consider that because this was her home. To her it was a safe space, and she didn't want to even think about somebody pulling that crap on her. Yet it was a hard conclusion to avoid. She had no idea if this guy Declan was verifiable, but he had given her a card. While he was still outside, she quickly made a phone call.

When a woman answered, Carly clarified who she was and what she was calling about. "Yes, that's Declan," the woman confirmed on the other end. "He's been investigating this case for us. I understand you were hurt when he got there."

"Apparently. Honestly I don't have any memory of it."

"That can be caused by any number of things," the woman noted, her tone sympathetic and calm. "If you want to talk to me at any point, just give me a call. My name is Kat."

Surprised at the invitation, Carly frowned. "Well, right now, I'm more interested in making sure I didn't let a serial killer make me a cup of tea," she replied in a half-joking manner.

"A serial killer who came to your rescue?" the woman

asked, with a note of humor. "I can assure you that Declan is safe, and he's very concerned about you. The man he saw as he approached might have been the one who attacked you. Do you have any way to verify whether there was an intruder in your home? Like a security system?"

"Oh, no. I don't have any cameras or anything like that. So no way to tell who might have been here."

"Right," Kat noted. "I can vouch for Declan at least, so that's not a point of concern."

"I'm glad to hear that," Carly replied. "He's coming back in, so I'll hang up now." She placed her phone on the table, picked up her tea, and sipped it, as Declan walked back into the house.

He shook his head. "No sign of the dog."

She closed her eyes and pinched the bridge of her nose. "I don't know where she's gone then. I thought she and I were starting to be friends."

"That doesn't mean that she left on her own volition," he reminded her.

Her eyelids flew open. "Yet the man you saw didn't have a dog with him, right?" she demanded.

"No, he didn't, none that I could see, and there was nothing with him when he went down the road."

She stared off in the distance. "It just doesn't make any sense."

"Well, it will make sense eventually. We just haven't gotten to the truth of it yet."

"Maybe," she replied doubtfully. "But why would anybody go after the dog? I was working on her, training her to become a therapy dog. Her disposition is perfect for it. I call her Shelby, and she's just been a beauty to work with."

"That's good. That's a huge part of why I'm here, to

ensure she'll be okay with you."

She winced. "Right, I'm not anybody who actually applied to adopt one, am I?"

"No, but we end up with a lot of cases where circumstance change and where the dogs have ended up in a completely different place than where they were originally intended to go," he shared with her. "It's not far off to consider that she could be perfectly happy with you."

She brightened. "When you get a chance to meet her, you'll see that she's really a sweetheart. She does really well with a lot of different people."

"Any reason you can think of as to why somebody may have kidnapped her for their own use?" he asked curiously.

"No, not at all," she muttered, "but you can never really tell with people."

"That's very true, but that would also mean we had two separate incidents, all within a very short span of time."

"Right." She frowned. "I'm not sure that's very logical."

"It's not. Not at all," he confirmed, as he studied her.

"I must really look horrific." She flushed. "You haven't taken your eyes off my head."

"There's fresh blood," he noted, by way of explanation.

She nodded, then held up the washcloth in her hand. "I was trying to clean off the dried blood."

"Well, you've managed to get it bleeding again." He stood and came around to look at the wound. "It doesn't look any worse though."

"Well, that's good," she muttered. "I don't n things getting any worse just now."

"No, but we need to find the War Dog, and you don't have any cameras that I can see."

"No, I don't, but it's never been an issue before."

"Well, it might be time to reconsider."

"They're expensive though, and I wouldn't have a clue what kind of a system to put in. I just feel that I would be living in fear all the time, if I had such a system to tend to."

"Living in fear is different than respecting the reality that the rest of the people in our world aren't always as nice as we would like them to be," he murmured.

She groaned. "Now that's true." She considered her history and winced. "I probably should have put something in already."

"Well, that's another question I wanted to bring up," he added. "When you spoke to Badger or Kat a few days ago—"

Carly looked at him, startled. "Kat, that's the woman I talked to on the phone just now."

Declan studied her and then nodded slowly. "If you called her, then, yeah, that would make sense. But I think you spoke with Badger the other day, who also noted that you sounded scared."

She tightened her lips together. "I'm not sure *scared* is quite the word I would use."

"What word would you use then?" he asked.

She stared off in the distance. "*Unnerved,* maybe."

"Okay, now we're splitting hairs," he pointed out calmly, with a bit of a smile. "What is it that has you feeling unnerved?"

She winced. "God, that just sounds stupid."

"Maybe a little, but let's get past the semantics and figure out what's going on here. Obviously something is going on."

"I don't even know really." She stared at him. "Honest to God, I didn't realize my life was such a mess, and, now, with you here, all kinds of issues are being highlighted."

"It kind of makes sense though. You were scared before I ever got here, which is why I am concerned that an intruder likely attacked you. So, tell me why you're scared?"

She slowly closed her eyelids. "It doesn't have anything to do with the dog."

"Meaning, I can butt out?"

She flushed. "Now I sound like a bitch, which, considering we don't know how long I would have lain on this floor if you hadn't come in to look after me …"

"That's not why I'm asking," he said softly. "However, in my world, you shouldn't have to live in fear. I came to help, and, if there's something I can do, I would like to."

She stared at him. "You came to help a War Dog. I'm hardly in the same category."

"I came to help," he stated in a flat tone. "And I try not to quibble about the details."

When she snorted at that, he grinned, and she was instantly charmed. Shaking her head, she smiled. "That smile of yours must get you into trouble all the time."

He looked at her in surprise, then frowned. "No trouble that I know of."

She shook her head. "Now that is a lie because that smile is lethal."

"Well, that might be," he agreed, "but it's never actually killed anyone to date."

"Ha. Maybe they just didn't see it for what it was. Anyway," she began, as she filled her teacup again from the pot, "as I mentioned, my troubles don't have anything to do with the dog."

"Okay, but you were attacked, and the War Dog is now missing. And, if those two things aren't connected, I need a little more of an explanation." He poured himself a coffee and sat back down at the table. Reaching across for her hand, he said, "Come on. Tell me."

She winced. "Nothing much to tell."

"Apparently there is," he disagreed. "You were scared before, but now the War Dog is missing. And, instead of jumping up and racing outside, it's almost like you have a good idea where she is."

"It's possible that I do know where she is, and it's not necessarily a bad thing."

"Explain, please."

"A high school kid nearby loves her dearly, and sometimes he takes her for a walk."

"So, you're thinking that, instead of being missing, she may be out on a walk?"

"It's possible. I've told him not to take her without letting me know, but he's got Down Syndrome, and, although he knows what he's supposed to do, he doesn't always manage to do it."

"Sounds like any kid to me."

She smiled. "His heart's in the right place. I know he loves the dog, and he would never hurt her."

"Okay, that's helpful, but it doesn't explain why you were afraid when you contacted Badger and Kat."

She stared at him. "You do know that those names don't really inspire confidence, right?"

He grinned. "Oh, but if you had met them, you wouldn't say that." Declan laughed. "They are two of the finest, most dedicated people you could ever imagine."

"Maybe so, but together, well, never mind. Anyway, I don't know if Deron would have taken the dog. It's possible that he has Shelby. It's also possible that it's something else. As far as being scared"—she hesitated a moment—"I had a series of break-ins, and somebody was leaving me very unpleasant gifts."

"Was the day you phoned in about the dog one of those days when you got an unpleasant gift?"

"No. It was a day I got an email that told me to move out of the area, to give up all the animals, and to find another way to make a living. Or else."

"What did they ultimately want?" he asked curiously.

She stared at him. "Won't you tell me that I'm imagining things or making too much out of it?"

"No." He shrugged. "A lot of lawless people are out there. So, if you've somehow connected with one of them, I'll be the first to say that I'm sorry, but we need to figure it out and get it to the police."

"I didn't contact the police when I discovered the first gift. I just ignored it. The second time I did call the police, and then, when I got the email threat in, I contacted them again, but apparently the email came from an account that's no longer open. As if it was just opened to send the email, then it was closed. I don't know who would be threatening me, or why, but somebody wants me to leave town."

"Have you made any enemies?"

"No, nobody I can think of." She turned her teacup around and around in her hand. She looked up at him, and, seeing an inquiring look, she shook her head. "No, I really haven't. You know how you think you're getting along just fine, then, every once in a while, something like this happens, and you realize you're not on the same wavelength as you thought you were? This has happened before, and I just kind of packed up and moved here." Enough bitterness filled her tone that she knew he would pick up on it.

"Okay, so that begs the question of who bothered you in

that other location?"

She stared at him, a grimace on her face. "I have racked my brain, trying to figure out who and why, but I just don't know."

"A few more details, please. What happened in your last location, and where was that?"

"California. I was there for about a year, before that New Mexico for about a year, and before that, New York."

"Why all the moving around?"

"Trying to find a place that felt like home," she replied. Then she frowned. "I'm sure you'll drag out this investigation, as I sincerely doubt you'll let it go. I don't think it can be related ..."

When she hesitated, he looked at her and raised an eyebrow. "But?"

"Both of my parents were murdered about six years ago," she shared. "The case was never solved."

CHAPTER 2

CARLY REALLY HATED that she had to bring it all back up. She'd done her best to try and keep all that tucked away and out of her current life. The pain never seemed to go away, and she doubted it would this time either. As she finally raised her gaze to look at Declan, he just stared at her. She shrugged. "Not too many people like me are in your world, I guess, *huh?*"

"I've dealt with a lot of deaths over the years," he told her. "What are your parents' names?" he asked.

"Henry and Susan Simpson."

Declan nodded. "Murder cases are always unpleasant. It's case specific, of course, and sometimes the pain is minimized, depending on the circumstances. However, it's always a shocking death for everybody involved and all too tragic. I want to believe in a world where a person has the right to live out their life on their own terms, without somebody else deciding to shorten it. Unfortunately, all too often, it doesn't end up that way."

She studied him quietly. "You're right, and, when it happens in your world, there's no way to ever get over it. Just when you think you are healing, something happens, and it pops up all over again."

He nodded. "Do you have any siblings?"

She shook her head. "No. It was just the three of us." At

that, her voice hitched at the remembered pain. She took a moment to compose herself. "I keep thinking it will get easier."

"And it will," he shared. "You're just not there yet."

"And somebody seems to want to keep dragging it up," she muttered.

"Do you think that's what this is all about?"

"I don't know." She closed her eyelids and bit her lip. Reopening them, she stared straight into his smoky gray eyes. "I just told you that I didn't think it was connected, and yet, as I sit here, I wonder how it couldn't be."

"Do you have any idea who killed your parents?"

"No, not a clue. I was away in college, and it had nothing to do with me. I didn't have any bad relationships, no drug or alcohol issues, nothing that could have caused anyone in my world to get to my parents and attack them," she stated. "Not understanding what happened with them kept me from making any progress for the longest time. I just didn't know how to function because I kept expecting to see boogeymen around every corner."

"And now?"

"The police tend to think I'm neurotic and make things up," she noted bitterly. "They don't really see that I am being all that cohesive in my explanations. And maybe they're right. Maybe I'm out to lunch. I don't even know anymore." She sighed.

"And that's the first thing that comes to mind," he muttered. "Any chance that somebody is just gaslighting you to make it seem like you're psychotic?"

She snorted. "I wouldn't be at all surprised."

"So, the fact that you have the dogs here, does that mean you started therapy animals for yourself?"

She nodded and smiled. "I did. I needed the comfort of not being alone, the comfort of having them here, especially when I had a panic attack. Of course that just confirms my instability, as far as the cops are concerned."

"Doesn't matter what they believe," Declan noted. "They still need to do their jobs and to look after you and into anything that might be happening in your world, regardless of whether or not you get panic attacks because your parents were murdered. Jesus, that would have almost anybody getting panic attacks. So, stop worrying about how you appear to others, and let's get to the bottom of what's going on here."

"Is there really a bottom? It seems like it's just been an endless emotional pit," she muttered.

"I understand why you would say that, but, in my world, there is an end to these things. So, let's see if we can find out what the end is. First, I need to figure out where the War Dog is."

She frowned at that, pulled out her phone, quickly made a call, and put it on Speaker. "Hello, Penny. Does Deron have Shelby?" Carly looked up at Declan and smiled.

"He took her to the dog park again. I thought you knew," Penny noted, with a groan. "I'm so sorry."

"I can't have him taking the dog without asking me first. I actually have somebody here from the war department checking up on Shelby. Imagine my surprise to find her gone."

At that, Penny gasped. "Oh my gosh. I'm so sorry. I'll send him right over."

"Could you please make sure he comes straightaway, so I don't have to go chasing him down? I got a bit of a head injury today, and I'm not in great shape."

"Oh gosh, we'll be right there," Penny replied.

Putting down her phone, Carly looked over at Declan, pleased when she saw his shoulders relax.

"Good. That's great news. One less thing I have to sort out."

She winced. "I'm sorry. You surely got more than you bargained for today. The other issues aside, it was bad enough to have you come all this way only to find that the neighbor took the dog without permission."

"Sometimes that happens, although it's a first for me."

She gave him a half smile. "It shouldn't be long before they get here, so you'll finally get to meet Shelby."

"You really like her, *huh*?"

"She's beautiful, and I don't really want to give her up right now."

"Well, she wasn't much help if the neighbor came in and took her without your permission. While having that kind of dog would be a good opportunity for you to have some protection, you'll need to put your foot down to make it a proper arrangement."

"I know, and believe me. I've thought of that. I'm just not sure how to get Deron to understand that he can't do this."

"A firm hand?"

"Not happening with me obviously, and, although his mother loves him very much, she's not able to produce a reliably firm hand either."

When a knock came on the door, she got up, took a step, then swayed in place for a moment.

"*Uh-oh. Here. Let* me help. Sit back down, and I'll go let them in." He walked to the front door, flung it open, and frowned at the young man standing there, holding the leash to the War Dog. Declan took the leash from him. "Young man, did you take this dog without asking?"

At that, Deron stepped back ever-so-slightly, turning to his mom.

She frowned at her son. "Tell him the truth."

Deron looked back at him and nodded. "I just took her down to the dog park," he replied immediately. "Shelby and I love to play in the dog park."

"That's nice, but today was a day that Carly needed the dog here. I can't have you taking Shelby away without permission. Do you understand?"

Deron again first looked at his mom, then back at him, and slowly nodded. "I did wrong?"

"You did wrong," Declan confirmed, with a nod. "You can do right next time though."

At that, Deron reached down to pet her. "I really like to take her for walks," he told Declan, a smile trying to shine through.

"That may be, but that's not appropriate, not right now." Declan asked the mother, "May I speak with you for a moment?"

Her gaze surprised, she told her son, "Deron, you can get started for home now, while I talk to him for a minute."

🐾

Carly heard the conversation from the kitchen, and she wondered at Declan's ability to handle Deron so easily. She slowly got up and walked into the living room. Immediately

Declan looked at her and frowned. She frowned right back. "Thanks for bringing her home, Deron," Carly called out, as she bent down to give Shelby a greeting.

Deron turned and walked away, his shoulders slumped.

"You don't have to tell Penny," she murmured to Declan.

"Yes, I do. It's really important that she understands why we have to do this." He looked over at Deron's mother, then confirmed that Deron was out of earshot. "Carly was attacked today," he told Penny. "Inside her own home."

"What?" Penny exclaimed, her hand going to her mouth. She looked at Carly and gave her the once-over, immediately seeing the dried blood and the look on her face. "Oh, of course. The dog would have protected you."

"Not only that but Declan came to see the War Dog, and, when it wasn't here, it just added to the confusion and chaos of trying to sort out what happened," Carly explained. "I don't want Declan taking Shelby back on behalf of the war department, so I really cannot have Deron taking her like that. It has to stop."

Penny immediately nodded, over and over again. "I'm so sorry. He's really a handful."

"I know that, and I know how challenging it is. I just don't want to put up a security system. I can't afford it, and I can't put extra locks on everything. I also know this dog can jump, if she wants to leave. But the bottom line is that I need to know she'll be here when I need her," she added.

Penny kept nodding her head. "You don't know who attacked you?"

"No." Carly sighed. "Apparently it was a tall male, dressed all in black, and he walked down the street afterward."

"I haven't even been home all morning. I'm so sorry," Penny said. "Deron always gets in trouble the most when I'm not around. That's the only time he starts deciding things on his own. The trouble is, his decisions aren't necessarily the best ones."

"Well, they're the best for him," Carly noted in a wry tone.

"Yeah, just not always the best for everybody else. It's been so hard since his father died."

"I get that. I really do. I just don't know what the solution is."

Penny squared off her shoulders. "It's not your problem. He's my son. I'll try to figure out how I can get through to him. You take care of yourself now." At that, Penny turned and walked away.

As Declan closed the door, Carly looked up at him. "You handled Deron with a fairly experienced hand," she noted. "Have you dealt with special-needs people before?"

"Not like that, no, but part of the problem is he thinks he can do whatever he wants, and nobody gets to do that, not when it comes to impacting other people's property, particularly a War Dog like this." Declan bent down in front of Shelby and spent a few minutes enjoying just being in her world.

"The problem with Shelby is, now that she's no longer in the military, she seems to just love everybody," Carly added. "I heard that sometimes they train that out of them, so I was a little worried when I first ended up with her."

"You never did tell me how you got Shelby," he noted.

"I found her on the highway. She came to me quite willingly. I searched for owners but couldn't find anyone, and, when I took her in to the vet for a checkup, he didn't say anything. But I know one of the girls there, and she told me later that, when they ran a scan, it came up as a War Dog. I realized that I probably had something I didn't have any right to, and, as much as I would love to keep her, that doesn't mean I get to."

Declan nodded. "Yeah. Just like with Deron, there are some requirements to be maintained."

"I know, which is why I reached out."

"So that brings me back to how Badger picked up on the fact that you were terrified."

She nodded. "Yes, I was, but I'm hoping that it's past tense now. I haven't had anything since the threatening email saying that I needed to leave."

"Well, nothing but a knock on the head. But back to the email. Was any particular reason given?"

"No, and the cops didn't seem to think that they could come up with anything that would help either."

He nodded. "I'd like to see the email." When she hesitated, he added, "Unless you have a reason I shouldn't."

"I don't. I just really hate to open up all that again. It's pretty depressing."

"I get it, but I wouldn't want you getting hurt any more than you already have been. I do have some experience in this area, plus an organization behind me, all with skills and resources beyond what the local police would have access to," he explained. "So, if it's all the same to you, I'd really like to take a look at that email."

She raised her hands in mock surrender, then gave Shelby one last cuddle. "Fine. I need to sit back down again anyway."

"How about the living room this time," he suggested.

She looked around. "Sure. Just grab my laptop from the

kitchen counter, would you?" As she made her way to a big soft chair in the living room, Shelby stayed close beside her, whining into her hand. "I know. You weren't here with me. I could have used you." As Declan returned with the laptop, she asked. "Would Shelby really be a help if I'm attacked?"

He nodded. "Yeah, very much so. And, by the looks of it, she's obviously quite close to you."

"Well, she loves everybody really. I'm not sure she loves me any more than anybody else."

"Ah." Declan smiled and reached down and stroked her beautiful coat. "How long have you had her?"

"A couple weeks now," she said, opening her laptop and signing in.

"And how long have the threats been going on?"

She looked up at him in surprise. "A bit longer than that, I think."

"So, not because of the dog then?"

She stopped, stared, and then shook her head. "I'll have to look it up, but I don't think so. And why would anybody want me to leave town just because I've picked up a shepherd?"

"I'm not sure, but why would anybody want you to leave town in the first place?"

"I've thought about that, but I just don't have any answers."

"Well, ... we'll get them," Declan stated.

She frowned at him. "You sound so sure."

"In my world, it helps a lot to step forward with a confident hand. If I help you out with this, you won't be a single woman living alone and targeted."

At his words, she stopped scrolling through her emails, studying him. "I guess that's really what it is, isn't it?"

"Too often, that's exactly what it is. They find out somebody lives here alone, and either they're after something that you know about or they're just here to torment their victim. But the next step could be anything from breaking and entering again to something worse."

"Such as?"

"Another attack," he said instantly. "Just because you feel that you're safe here doesn't mean that you actually are."

"*Great.* I would very much like to be safe."

"Of course you would." He chuckled. "Yet the only way we'll get there is to get to the bottom of this, one way or the other."

"Right." She shook her head. "Here's the email." She flipped around her laptop, so he could see it. "It doesn't say a whole lot."

"No, but just look at that picture."

She knew what he meant. A picture of a beheaded cat.

"Is that a photograph of a cat you actually know?"

"I hope not. I've never really understood why anybody has to hurt cats."

"I don't know why, but they seem to be a favorite victim for sick assholes to prey on," he muttered. "In your case, as much as I hate to say it and wouldn't want to see it, dogs would make more sense."

"That's what I thought too," she agreed, "since I'm looking after and training dogs."

"I know, but again the mind that would do something like this is sick to begin with."

"See? We don't really even know that he actually did this. For all we know, it's a picture he picked up from somewhere on the internet."

He nodded. "Good point. It still doesn't give us any answers though, does it?"

She shook her head, and then gasped, reaching for her head. "I have got to stop moving my head so much."

"Let's get you to bed, so you can lie down," he offered.

"No, I really don't want to give in to it. I have chores to do, and I'm not ready to sleep."

"Not ready to sleep or too scared to close your eyes?" he asked her.

"I didn't say that," she protested immediately, but he gave her a knowing glance.

"You didn't have to."

DECLAN FROWNED AT her. "Look. You don't know me. I get that. You don't know if you can trust me. I get that too. I'm hoping that, by phoning my bosses, you got some kind of a character reference and that you know that I'm not here to hurt you."

"I did that, ... but knowing it intellectually doesn't mean that I'm necessarily ready to trust you quite so completely just yet. Oddly enough I made the call, but I didn't get a photo confirmation."

He chuckled, pulled out his phone, took a selfie, and sent it to Kat, with a text request to please verify that it was most certainly him.

Kat immediately sent back a question mark and then a text. **Yes, this is you**.

Declan held it up for Carly to see.

She sighed. "I'm being foolish, aren't I?"

"No. I'm actually glad to see you pushing back a little. But ultimately you'll have to make a decision to trust me, or we'll have a little trouble moving forward to the next step."

Her eyes widened. "What's the next step?"

"I want you to go to bed, if not for the rest of the evening, then at least for a nap or just to get you to lay down," he stated. "I plan to bunk down here for the night. One, because of that head injury, and, two, because—until I figure out what is going on and just how dangerous it is—I don't want to leave you alone. And you did tell me that you live alone, something else you should probably be more aware of."

"That's true. I live here alone, except for my dogs. Just remember though, whatever I may have said earlier, I'm pretty sure I wasn't exactly in my right mind, since I was waking up from being unconscious."

"That's a good point," he agreed. "I'm quite concerned about that head injury morphing into something that's a little more serious."

"I don't think it will," she said. "It hurts, but it's not any worse than it was."

"No, but that doesn't mean that something is not going on underneath."

"You can stay down here for the night. ... I should be thanking you because, at the moment, my world feels a bit too scary to continue alone. It also feels odd, relying on a stranger."

"Exactly. That's why it's so great that I'm not a stranger and that you've already checked out my credentials," he reminded her, cheerful now that he knew she wouldn't fight him on staying. "The problem is, something is obviously going on, and we'll have to sort it out, but it'll take at least a day or two. It's not as if this can get solved immediately, unless you have some idea who's behind it, and then I can get the cops to go shake them down."

"Which won't happen because I don't know who it is," she declared, raising her hands in frustration. Then she groaned and winced. "I have to stop talking, and I have to stop making rapid movements of any kind." She slowly got to her feet and grabbed the nearby doorjamb, moving toward the stairs. "I will go lie down. You do you."

"What about the dogs?"

"Oh, can you go let them in?"

He nodded and walked out to the kitchen. When he stepped out and opened the gate, they all came barreling inside. She crouched down on the bottom steps and gave them cuddles. "I'm sorry, guys. I should have let you in earlier."

He looked over at her. "Do they all get along?"

"Pretty well, so if you could just fill up their dry food bowl, that will do for tonight. It won't hurt them to not get treats."

He laughed. "Are you asking me or them about that? From the looks of things, I'm pretty sure they would beg to differ."

"You could be right," she murmured, "but that'll take a little more energy than I have at this moment."

"Hey, I'm here to help. Do they get wet food?"

She hesitated and then shrugged. "Sure, why not. It would keep them calm and keep us in our routine."

"And a routine is important," he murmured. "Particularly for animals that are worried about you."

She quickly gave him further instructions and then announced, "I'm going upstairs."

"Do you want a hand?" Declan asked.

"Nope. I don't want a hand. I just want to go upstairs,

lie down, and forget about the mess my world is in right now," she muttered. As he watched from the bottom of the stairs, she slowly made her way up, the dogs at her feet the whole way.

"You'll be lucky if they don't trip you on the way," he called up.

"It wouldn't be the first time," she noted. "It's part of the training I have to continuously work on. They get so excited, and they just want to be part of it all."

"And yet respect says they stay behind and you go first."

"Sure, and you know the thing about respect is, you've got to stay on it all the time."

He smiled as the dogs came back downstairs, investigating his presence in their home. He crouched to greet them all, trying to get to know each one of them. "It would be nice to know who you each are, but I don't know your names yet," he told them. "So I'll do the best I can, and hopefully none of you will get too offended." He checked his watch and realized it was probably their dinnertime, so, following Carly's instructions, he fed them all in the kitchen.

"When you guys are ready, you can go on up to her bed. You probably all pile on top, don't you? Maybe she'll be lucky and get some sleep before that." He would need food at some point, plus Carly would benefit from having something too. He hesitated, wondering whether he should just order in or try to make something simple here. He didn't want to leave her alone to make a store run.

He opened the fridge and found the fixings for spaghetti sauce and also a package of spaghetti noodles sitting on the counter. He hesitated and then shrugged. "Okay, spaghetti it is. If you hate it, I'll gladly replace your ingredients." And with that, quite happy in the kitchen, he fussed about with chopping onions, while he got the meat started, then poked around until he found garlic and spices.

Once he had the pasta sauce simmering, he put on a big pot of water to cook up a good amount of pasta, knowing spaghetti was always great the second day.

The dogs didn't seem to have any problem with his presence, which was the only thing he'd been concerned about. They all seemed to be quite content with the situation. From the looks of it, two of them had gone upstairs already, as had the War Dog. However, as Declan went around the corner to the bottom of the stairs, he found Shelby lying by the bottom step, her gaze ever watchful. She'd chosen a position in the hallway, where she could keep an eye on both the stairs and the kitchen.

"Smart dog," he noted, as he bent down and scratched her.

She immediately rolled over and gave him her belly.

"Definitely not a whole lot of scary War Dog in there right now." Declan chuckled. He'd seen a lot of the work the War Dogs could do when they were out in action, and it was amazing. It was also quite daunting to realize how much training they had during those times to make them understand the job that needed to be done, and yet they went at it willingly each and every time.

He also noticed that Shelby didn't appear to be injured in any way, which was a good thing. It wasn't always that way, as some War Dogs came back missing limbs, and some even had to be put down because their injuries were too severe. But thankfully, lots of times when they retired, they were out of that life and became these couch potatoes, which he highly suspected Shelby would be. However, if she took to people like Deron so easily, which he knew a lot of animals would, then maybe Shelby did have the temperament to become a great therapy dog.

He didn't know what kind of training was required or what kind of people Carly needed the dogs to bond with, but, based on what he'd seen so far, Shelby was pretty laid-back.

By the time the pasta was done, he drained it, put it back in the pot, with a bit of butter, to keep it all warm and then called up the stairs. "Hey, are you awake?" He heard a muffled sound. Stepping over Shelby at the base of the stairs, he walked up the stairs, calling out, "I'm on my way up."

"I'm here," she called back from the master bedroom. He stepped into the bedroom and looked at her critically. She was covered by a deep blue blanket, the room dimly lit, so he didn't see more than her face and an outline of her body.

"You don't look too bad now," he said.

"Right, nothing like a good nap." She rolled over and pushed herself up to lean against the headboard. "I have to admit though, the head still doesn't feel too great."

"It won't feel great for a while yet," he murmured. "I was wondering if you were hungry. It might do you some good to eat a bit."

She stared at him. "What are you thinking?"

"Well, I took some liberties, while you were snoozing," he admitted, with a wry look. "I figured, if it upset you, I could always just go replace what I used."

"What are you talking about?"

He shrugged. "I have a spaghetti sauce simmering, and the pasta just came off, so I came to see if you wanted to come down and eat."

She blinked. "You cooked?"

He opened his eyes wide. "Yes, and I quite enjoyed it." He chuckled at that. "So, are you up for trying my spaghetti, or am I eating it myself?"

She laughed. "Hey, if somebody else wants to cook, I'm totally up for eating." She swung her legs round the side of the bed and sat there for a moment, then slowly got up. She immediately grabbed the headboard. "Oh, maybe I'm not quite as okay as I thought I was."

"No, probably not. When you've been lying down, it's not uncommon to get dizzy when you stand up."

She waited a few minutes. "Well, the room has stopped moving, so I guess I'll try it again."

"That's good." He watched carefully as she took several steps toward him.

"I think I'm okay," she said.

He reached out a hand. "Hold on to me, and I'll help you down the stairs." And that's what they did.

When she got down to the bottom, the dogs completely surrounded them, until she gave several orders, and they all fell back, giving her space.

"That helps," he noted.

"They're actually quite well trained, but they know something is wrong."

"Of course they do," Declan agreed. "Animals are very intuitive." With Carly now sitting at the table, he quickly served her a portion of pasta. "How much sauce do you like?"

"Lots," she replied immediately. "I do love sauce."

"You might not like this one though," he added, then smirked. "But it's the only sauce you've got right now, so you are kind of stuck with it." Then he placed a plate down in front of her.

"There's some parmesan in the fridge," she told him.

He was surprised when he looked and spied a large block of it. "That's awesome. Do you have a grater I could use?"

"I do." She pointed out the cupboard it was in, and he grated some on top of her spaghetti. "That's good, thank you." She stared at her plateful, getting closer to sniff it. "Wow, this smells heavenly."

"It's my grandmother's recipe." Declan lifted his glass of water, clinked it with hers, and said, "Enjoy."

She smiled. "You know what? This day has been full of surprises. As crazy as it's been, there was never a time when I expected it would end like this."

"Well, hopefully it's not a bad thing." Declan dug his fork in and twirled it around. Lifting a load of pasta on it, he took a big bite. With a smile, he nodded. "It's really good. At least, this is how it's supposed to taste anyway." He watched as she picked up a much smaller bite.

When she tasted it, her eyes widened. "Oh, wow, this is way better than mine."

"I doubt it, but thanks."

She smiled. "Well, my mother didn't cook," Carly shared, "so everything I've learned has been the hard way."

"I've learned a lot from my grandmother—and my parents. They all live back in California, so it's not all that hard to call them up if I need a recipe or something. But most of the recipes I have committed to memory because they're the ones I use over and over again."

"Those are the best kind," she agreed. "You can count on them and can trust them to be there when you need to call on them."

"Unlike people, *huh?*"

"Unlike a lot of people, yeah," she said.

"Sounds like a story or two are in there somewhere."

"Not good stories. It was really hard when my parents passed away, and, because it was murder, everybody questioned by the police seemed to think that maybe I had accused them or something. Plus everybody at college ditched me because I was uncomfortable to be around. I never knew what to say and burst into tears at the drop of a hat. You know, that kind of a thing. I understood their reactions, yet it just made for a very lonely pathway."

"You didn't have any really close friends?"

"No, other than a steady boyfriend, not really. I was really focused on school and trying to get ahead. I was actually doing extra classes, so I had a heavier class load than those around me. I didn't have time for all the partying that everybody else seemed to do." She frowned. "There was an incident on campus that blew up and added to all the stress and chaos. That didn't help either."

"What happened?"

"*Ugh*, what a mess. There were a couple rapes on campus, and my boyfriend at the time was picked up as a suspect. I knew he didn't do it, but everybody else assumed that he had—or at least was involved somehow. He was released without too much of a problem," she added. "However, after that, it was as if I was always being watched and people were wondering why I was with a rapist. It got kind of ugly and really turned me when it comes to people and their opinions."

"Anything that makes you the gossip topic of the week is unpleasant," Declan stated, with a nod. "Just remember that the people who don't count are the ones who would judge you, and the people who do count are the ones who wouldn't. Can't say I ever experienced anything like that though."

"No, that alone was pretty rough," she admitted. "My parents were murdered about two years after that, and I already knew how people would talk. Plus, as I mentioned, I was awkward to be around and overly emotional. People didn't know how to handle it, and, well, it felt safer for me to step back, before it had a chance to get any worse."

"That's a quickly learned lesson on your part, although some of those people might well have been there to lend some support."

"Maybe, but I probably didn't give them much of a chance. I was also dealing with shock and denial, trying to figure out what was going on. The police kept asking me all these questions, and, as the only child, I inherited everything, so that made them suspicious all over again. Thankfully my extended class schedule I kept made it relatively quick and easy to verify my alibi through both witnesses and campus security cameras. Without that, I don't know what they would have done." Carly shook her head, looking down at her plate sadly.

"It's a sick world when they look at the kids for killing the parents, and yet it happens," he murmured.

"I know, and that's what they tried to tell me too. It just seemed so far-fetched. I loved my parents and would do anything to have them back again," she whispered, tears flooding her eyes. She brushed them away impatiently. "Wow, this has really been quite the day." She twirled up another fork of spaghetti.

"You're tired still, and overwrought. I know for a fact that you're stressed. Plus you've still got shock running through your system, and we're bringing up painful subjects, so any and all of it explains the emotions."

She gave him half a smile. "You're a nice man."

"Why? Because I understand that life isn't always easy?"

"Because you keep giving me opportunities to just relax and to not feel that I have to be on my guard all the time."

"I'm hoping that maybe you won't feel you have to be responsible all the time."

"Is that what it is?" She shrugged. "I don't even know that I feel responsible, but, because I wasn't at home when my parents died, I guess I feel guilty, because had I been there, maybe I could have done something to stop it."

"Chances are, you would have been killed as well. You know that, right?"

"I do know that, and the cops tried to tell me the same thing. Add to all that the fact that you've just lost everything important, and then suddenly you're expected to look after a nasty crime scene that was left in the kitchen and deal with all the executor stuff at the same time. Meanwhile you're not able to bury their bodies because the police wanted to do extra testing, autopsies and all the rest of it." She swallowed back more tears and sighed. "I ended up losing the rest of that school year. I did return the following year to finish because I only had the one semester left, and it was something to focus on that had some structure. After that? Well, I just didn't know."

"*Huh?*"

She shrugged. "I never did go into business as planned because I didn't know quite what to do. It wasn't a normal life anymore for me," she muttered.

He listened as she talked, knowing some of it was just a need to talk about anything, and the other part was the need to talk to somebody who might understand and could at least help her out a little. "Do you think that anything to do with college could have been related to your parents' murder?"

"I don't know how," she stated, looking at him in surprise. "I don't know why it would."

"No, I don't know either," he murmured, "but again we're just trying to get answers to all those questions about what caused the trouble."

"There are so many holes instead of answers all the time that it makes it difficult."

"It does, but, hey, you look like you're holding up all right."

"Maybe, though I'm not so sure about that at times. It just seems everything is a mess."

"Give yourself a little credit," he said. "It looks like you have an appetite at least, and that's a good sign."

"I do have an appetite." She frowned, looking down at her plate in surprise. "I honestly didn't realize I was that hungry, but that was really good."

"It was, if I do say so myself." Declan smiled at her almost empty plate. "It makes for a pretty good meal." He relaxed in his chair for a moment. "I'll do the dishes and let you sit for a little bit. Take your time, but then it's off to bed again."

She groaned. "I guess, but here's hoping for a better day tomorrow."

"That's the plan," he agreed, with a smile. "But first, we need to get you feeling better. Then tomorrow maybe you'll have a new opinion on life in general." With that, he got up and started collecting the dishes.

CHAPTER 3

CARLY STARTED TO get out of bed the next morning and froze at her first movement.

"Oh my God," she whispered, grateful no one was nearby to hear her. She had no idea how sore her body would be after that attack yesterday. Otherwise she would never have moved so abruptly. The dogs woofed around her ankles, wondering what her problem was. She reached down to cuddle them, even wincing at that simple movement.

"I know, guys. I'm getting there. Honest to God, I really am trying to get up and move." She knew that every step, every movement would be more of the same, but there was no way to avoid it. She had to get up and go to the bathroom.

Groaning out loud, but as softly as she could so her house guest wouldn't hear, she stood, then using the newel post of her bed, she headed to the bathroom. There she used the facilities, and, by the time she finished washing her hands, she was ready to take a serious look at her face.

"Well, it's actually not as bad as I expected," she muttered. Then she turned ever-so-slightly to see the back of her head and winced. The dried blood had her hair clumped together in an unruly mess, obscuring the wound underneath. She stared at the shower, wondering if it was safe to try. The last thing she wanted was to run into trouble and have to call for help to get out.

Giving herself a mental assessment, she decided that a shower was worth the attempt. She would just take it slow. And, if she had to sit for a while, she would sit. With that decided, she turned on the water, stripped down, and stepped under the warm spray. It took her several attempts to get everything out of her hair, and she tried to ignore the fact that now fresh blood streamed down the drain.

When she shut off the water, she felt surprisingly strong. Buoyed by that success, she grabbed a towel, wrapped it around her, grabbed a second one for her hair, then headed back to her bedroom. It took a bit longer to dry herself and to get dressed, before she headed downstairs. When she made it into the kitchen, Declan sat at the kitchen table, studying her intently.

"I'm fine," she said, noticing the concern in his eyes. "I'm actually feeling better than I expected."

"And better than you ought to with a thumping like that," he added, with a half smile.

She understood what he meant. "Maybe so, but no way I could stay in bed any longer. Laying around is not my style."

"No, it's not mine either." He studied her for a moment. "I must say, you are looking quite a bit better." Then he frowned, hopped up, and reached out to check her head. "The shower just brought up some more bleeding where the scabs were disturbed, but at least the shampoo should have kept it clean." He grabbed a paper towel and dabbed at her scalp. "It's just welling up a little, but, if we catch it now, it won't clump up in your hair again."

"That would be nice," she muttered. "It's amazing how sore my scalp is."

He nodded. "That's one of the reasons I never understood all these fancy hairdos women put their hair in. I imagine, by the end of the day, your whole head hurts."

"It can, but, once you're used to it, it's not that bad. It does happen though, especially after a long day. So, yeah, it can get pretty painful."

Once he was done, he shooed her toward the table. "Let me get you some coffee."

"I'm hardly an invalid," she protested, but it was like arguing with a wall, so she found herself sitting down at her own table, a cup of coffee immediately placed in front of her.

"I'm staying in your house, so I can earn my keep and do something for you."

She smiled at his attempt at humor. "Hey, you made the coffee. That's always a good start."

"I also fed the dogs again," he shared.

She looked at him in surprise, then glanced at the microwave, which told her the time. "Wow, I didn't expect it to be so late. And the fact that I left my cell phone upstairs and didn't even think about the time says a lot about where my head is at."

"It does, indeed, but it's all good. Everything looks normal."

Then Carly noted Shelby on the kitchen floor, her tail wagging as she looked at her, but she had yet to get up. "Did you tell her to stay there?"

"Yeah, I didn't want you to get overwhelmed." He immediately gave a hand signal, and the dog bolted toward Carly.

She laughed as she got the greeting of her life. "Oh, I do love this animal," she exclaimed, with a bright smile. "There is just so much joy and exuberance in her whole demeanor."

"She does appear to be very happy and settled here,"

Declan stated. "Except for visitors who keep coming in and out, without asking permission."

"You mean Deron again?"

He nodded. "I do."

"Did he come already this morning?"

"He came to the door and asked, and I told him that you were still asleep and that he could come back later."

She smiled. "That's not a bad way to handle it. I hope you were gentle."

"I was. He did what we asked of him, and, although it wouldn't work right now, maybe in the future it wouldn't be so bad if Deron came over unannounced and took Shelby to the park without your knowledge."

"Well, I'm glad to hear that," she said, "because the two of them are quite happy together."

"Sure, but, if you're planning on using her as a therapy dog, she and Deron need to know where the boundaries are because working dogs need to work."

"I get that," she stated. "I'm just surprised that you do."

"No need to be surprised," he replied. "I've been around working dogs like this all my life, at least my adult life."

"Yet, it's not what you do anymore?" she asked.

He looked over at her, lifted his pant leg.

For the first time, she realized he had a prosthetic. "Oh wow."

"It's just down at the ankle, but it's amazingly awkward and definitely keeps me out of active duty."

"So, you took a retirement?"

"Well, it was effectively a medical discharge, and I didn't want to go back unless I could do the active duty work I'd done before."

"Got it. I would never have noticed if you hadn't shown

me."

"No need to notice now either, since it doesn't change a damn thing."

"I agree. I can see that you are well-adjusted."

"I don't know that well-adjusted is the phrase I'd use. Nobody ever likes to be missing a limb," he added, "but I'm a realist, and that's just the way it is for me right now."

"What about the prosthetic?" she asked. "Are you responsible for procuring those?"

He smiled down at it. "This one actually came from my boss's wife, Kat, the woman you spoke to. She's a specialist in the field. Plus both she and Badger are missing limbs as well." Carly's jaw dropped, and he shrugged. "It's actually more common than you think."

"Maybe, it's just not very common in my world."

"No, but now you've touched up against the War Dog world, and most of us who are no longer in active duty service are out for a reason." He pointed to his prosthetic. "In my case, this is the reason."

"Any other injuries?" she asked curiously and then flushed. "Oh my God, I'm sorry. That was a very personal question. I apologize."

"I don't mind, and, yeah, there are few other things. I lost a kidney, and I've got quite a bit of scar tissue along my back. I've got bones that will never really work properly, but they're ribs and good enough to protect my lungs, so it's all good. I'm fine," he said cheerfully.

"I have a hunch that, even if you're not fine, you'll be fine regardless."

He looked at her in surprise and then burst out laughing. "Exactly. Only so many things in life you can argue with."

She looked around the kitchen. "Was everything calm overnight?"

"Meaning?"

"Meaning, were there any intruders about or any strange or unpleasant remnants left outside?"

"None that I saw," he told her. "I had all the dogs, including Shelby, out a couple times. I even took her out in the night, just checking the perimeter to ensure everything was okay."

"How did she take to that?" she asked curiously.

"With great joy." Declan laughed. "I'm hoping we can end up making her as much of a watchdog as you'll need."

"That would be nice too," she said. "I hadn't really considered it, but, after you worried about somebody coming into the house …"

"I was really hoping you had camera surveillance here."

"I don't. Yet it had been suggested."

"I'm surprised though, after your parents were murdered and all."

"I know, yet having cameras and a fancy security system didn't help them one bit."

He looked at her in surprise. "They had all that?"

She nodded. "They did, but they also lived alone, and my father thought it was a prudent thing to keep around."

"But did they use it?"

"That is a whole different story," she replied, with half a smile. "They did get to be a little cavalier about their lives."

"Of course they did," Declan agreed. "Like here for you, in a small town like this, it's easy to forget that the bigger world can intrude, even when we don't want it to. And people get complacent, no matter where they live."

"Ever since then, it was something I'd been very strict

about, and then I moved here and didn't really have the money anymore. In my world, things appeared to be much calmer, and over time I convinced myself that maybe I could test out a different way to live and see if I could do without the whole panicked idea of always being locked in."

"So, it's not so much that you really don't want a security system, you're just worried about becoming too dependent on it."

She tilted her head as she considered that. "Maybe. I think when something like that happens to you, you don't necessarily have clarity as to all the reasons behind the choices you make."

"Most people double up on security and lock themselves in."

"And maybe if that had made a difference with my parents, I would have done it too," she murmured, "but it didn't. So I guess I was seeing it as a false sense of security." She finished her coffee, but before she had a chance to stand up to get more, he was already up. "You don't have to wait on me."

He smiled and shook his head. "Hey, I'm just trying to be a good house guest."

"Oh, come on." She laughed at that. "I highly doubt that even occurred to you."

He looked at her, faking an injured smile. "Of course it did."

She smiled, then sank back a bit and looked hesitant. "Now that you've decided that the War Dog is adjusted and okay, is there any reason I can't keep Shelby?"

"I'll talk to Badger about it, but, if you're looking to get rid of me right now, it won't happen."

She stared at him, nonplussed. "Well, I wasn't trying to

get rid of you," she replied, when she found her voice again. "But I didn't know you were looking to stay for any particular reason."

"I'll stay because I'm still not sure what is happening here. For example, I still don't know if it's connected to the War Dog, which is the other thing that changed in your life recently."

She stared down at the dog, then looked at him in surprise. "I didn't even think of that. But you did question me on that earlier but I forgot..."

He grinned. "Which is why I did think of it. ... I just don't know whether somebody wants the dog from you, is looking to see what Shelby can do, or just doesn't like something about Shelby. Maybe he wants the War Dog taken away. Maybe he wants it shot. I don't know."

She looked at him with a horrified expression. "Now that is guaranteed to keep me from sleeping at night."

"People have strange reactions to War Dogs. Some, even hearing the phrase *War Dog*, freak out and think the animal is a weapon. Granted, they are trained to be weapons, defensive and offensive, but the key word there is *trained*. So, like for your therapy work, the military training alone that Shelby got earlier would make her a good candidate. Of course the personality of the retired War Dog must be evaluated."

Declan shrugged and continued. "Most of the time, War Dogs do well transitioning into retired civilian life. They're great, but I've seen a couple *people* who had less-than-pleasant experiences with these War Dogs while in military service and either blame the War Dogs or just saw them as an extension of an institution they hated."

"Good God." Carly immediately wrapped her arms

around Shelby. "She's far too beautiful to hate."

"People will still be people."

She winced. "No, I understand that part, and yet I've just been trying to forget it."

"Well, no way you can keep your head in the sand, not while knowing a man was in your home yesterday, at the same time you ended up unconscious with a head injury."

"I wish I had seen him," she mumbled. "Maybe I would have recognized him, you know?"

"You think?"

"I have no idea." She stared at him in surprise. "Yet I would like to think I would."

"You would feel better thinking I was making it up," he suggested.

She flushed. "That sounds foolish because that means a part of me thinks you're lying."

"Well, how about we don't call it lying, but maybe go with the possibility that I was mistaken instead."

She let out a breath. "Thank you for not being so sensitive, as some people might have been with this same conversation." She smiled as she shook her head.

"It's not that I'm *not* sensitive," he clarified, "but this is important."

"Oh, I'm all for that," she declared. "I have no idea how to stop this nightmare because I don't know what's going on."

"Which is why I spoke with my bosses about the murder case. We discussed it this morning, and I filled them in, and we talked about the potential of it somehow being connected to the War Dog."

"Which doesn't make any sense because I didn't have Shelby back then."

"Right," he agreed, with a smile. "That doesn't mean somebody hasn't decided the dog is now connected to whatever problem they have with you."

She just stared. "So, what did you and your bosses decide?" She didn't even know what to think about this. It was a huge relief to have him around. Yet, at the same time, that whole tendency to live in fear was something she didn't want to get back into again. But how could she not, especially when things kept happening?

"Basically we've decided that I should stay here for a few days, just to see if anything else comes up."

"And if not?"

"Then we reassess," he replied. "Obviously I can't stay here forever, but, if something is going on that puts you at risk, we won't leave you to fend for yourself."

She snorted. "I don't know why not. The rest of the world feels that way."

He smiled. "We're not like the rest of the world. We defend our own." And, with that, he got up. "Now, I was about to go make some pancakes. Are you up for that?"

She looked at him in surprise. "A house guest that's concerned about my safety, the welfare of my pets, and you cook." She shook her head. "So, why aren't you married?"

He looked back at her with half a smile. "Remember the foot?"

She stared at him, surprised. "Yeah, what about it?"

"Well, it might not be a big deal to you, but trust me. It's a big deal to a lot of women."

"You're kidding? None of that matters," she declared instantly, still mystified. "Good God, isn't that a little superficial to disregard the person inside?"

"Maybe. Yet I too was pulling back from anything serious. All the time I was in the service, I couldn't take the chance of leaving behind a family, since I was constantly traveling and in combat or other dangerous situations all the time," he explained. "Then, once I got injured and out of active duty and was recovering, I had one scenario where somebody I really liked came to visit me, took one look, and decided she didn't need an invalid in her world."

"That's cold. What happened then?"

"She took off." He shrugged, but she could sense the disquiet within him.

"I seem to remember some wise person telling me how the people who don't count are the ones who would judge you, and the people who do count are the ones who wouldn't."

He looked over at her, flashed a grin her way, and nodded. "Well, it's nice to know that it doesn't bother you and that you're not horrified by my prosthetic."

"Hell no," she stated forcefully. "No way it would bother me. Besides, my father was military too."

At that Declan froze, slowly turned to face her, stunned.

"What? It was years ago." She frowned at him, wondering what was up.

"Did he leave, retire or what?"

"Neither, as far as I know. He was still in the service around that time I think. Or maybe he left just before when I was in college," she said. "Why?"

"Did you happen to mention any of that to the detectives investigating your father's murder?"

She stared at him and then slowly shook her head. "No, I didn't. It never occurred to me."

"Do you know how long ago he was enlisted? Or where he served? Who his commander was? Anything?"

Again she stared at him in shock. "No, I really don't know any of that."

"Fine." He rubbed his face. "So, after breakfast, I want proper names, birthdates, and social security numbers or whatever you have, for both of your parents."

"Okay," she said, still confused, "but surely the cops would have looked all that up."

"It's hard to say if they went as far as checking for military service records. Maybe it's not connected at all, but it's definitely something I would prefer to check."

"I'm not saying to ignore it," she clarified. "I just never considered that it could be important." Then she shrugged. "He wouldn't talk about it at all."

"Wouldn't talk about what?"

"Any of the work he did in service. He would say something about that time in his life was in the past, and some things were better kept closed."

"You know something?" Declan nodded. "I agree with him on that to some degree. There are things that happen in our lives that we don't want to revisit, and sometimes the best way to do that is to close that door permanently." He sat down, faced her, and added, "However, if your father was involved in anything back then that came around in an ugly way and killed him, we need to know."

"Well, I hope you're wrong. I really do."

"I do too," he said. "On the other hand, if I'm not, it could open a whole new avenue of investigation, and maybe we could solve who killed your parents."

AFTER BREAKFAST HAD been cleared away, and the kitchen

tidied up, Declan sat down in the living room with his laptop and accessed several links that Badger had sent him. There wasn't any information of interest in her father's military records, but there was a record of several internal articles that he had accessed. Not for the first time, Declan wondered just what kind of access Badger and Kat had because it was certainly a huge help when it came to things like this.

He was halfway through when Badger phoned.

"I just got off the phone with a friend who knew her father in the military," Badger began.

"Do I need to go somewhere private?" Declan asked, looking around, but she was in the kitchen, fussing with something.

"No, just watch what you say."

"Okay, what's going on?"

"Her father was involved in a court-martial case and personally made several accusations of theft within the military. I have the details and records on the trial and the man who was convicted."

"That's interesting," Declan replied. "Are you thinking it might be related to … you know?"

"His death? Well, I'm not saying that it is, but it's definitely something we can't afford not to consider."

"Of course. That's the reason I called you in the first place."

"Exactly," he murmured. "Now, the thing is, the guy served his time and was released."

"When?"

"One year ago."

"Oh, wow, how long was he … away?" Declan looked around again, trying to see where Carly had gotten to, not wanting his end of the conversation to upset her.

"He was sentenced to twenty years, after being convicted of selling weapons to our enemies. At least that's how the case went down, and that added quite a bit more to his sentence. He was released early, in that he'd been a model prisoner while inside, though he had always maintained his innocence. However, when he left prison, he left with quite a chip on his shoulder."

"Ah, crap, if he got out a year ago, then he was incarcerated when they were murdered six years ago."

"Ironically he was released once for his father's funeral, then returned to complete his sentence."

"Don't tell me it was in the target range."

"Yep," Badger confirmed. "Of course he says he had nothing to do with anything, and he's still pretty bitter."

"Right, but the fact that he had time out for that funeral also makes it very difficult to give him a clean alibi."

"Exactly. He lives about three hours away from you."

"Really. Well, maybe I'll see if I can go talk to him."

"If you do, you may want to take her along. Apparently he knew her when she was younger and was always a big fan."

"But not necessarily now," Declan guessed, "not when you consider the fact that he spent twenty years in the can because of her father."

"I know, so use your judgment on that."

Declan got down as many of the salient details as he could, and then he added, "Send me any other information you have, and I'll talk to Carly about it."

When he hung up, he heard her voice from the kitchen doorway. "Talk to me about what?"

He sighed, quickly trying to think of the best way to fill

her in. "Your father was involved in a criminal case within the military," he shared. "Somebody close to him was stealing and selling goods to the enemy."

She winced. "You're talking about Dean, aren't you?"

He looked at her in surprise.

"Yeah, I did know about that. Another subject I was quite happy to ignore."

"And why is that?"

"Because I really liked Dean, and, when I found out he'd been convicted, I couldn't believe it. I wouldn't believe it."

"Well, Dean is out of prison and still swears he's innocent."

"I know my father was very convinced that he was anything but innocent," she stated. "It's one of the reasons why both my mom and I chose not to listen to my dad."

"Well, Dean got out a year ago, and Badger suggested I might want to go talk to him."

She stared at him in surprise. "What good would that do?"

He shrugged. "I'm not sure it will do any good at all, but you should know that he was also free on a funeral pass for a few days when your parents were murdered."

"What?" She gasped, staring at him. "Oh, good Lord." Her hand went to her mouth in shock.

He nodded. "The reason he was given that leave was because his father had died, and he was given the okay to go to the funeral. He was also a model prisoner the entire time."

"And that would be him," she agreed. "I really struggled with the fact that he supposedly had done this, and yet I didn't know any of the details."

"Your mother was in the military as well, right?"

"Yes, but not the same area. Although I don't really even

know what area either of them were in. They wouldn't talk about it much. However, Dean was somebody who used to come over all the time, and they considered him a friend. Toward the end, what I understood was that they thought he had used them for whatever it was he was doing, and that was something they found hard to forgive."

"Badger wanted to know whether you would want to go see Dean when I go."

She stared at him. "I don't know. … That could get very ugly."

"It could, no doubt, but it's also possible he might want to see you. Maybe he wants you to know the truth, or maybe he believes that he's innocent and would like to have somebody believe him."

"But, if he's innocent, that means my father was wrong," she muttered. "I don't know if I'm ready to deal with that."

"No, and I get that," Declan noted. "Yet if it's connected to the murders—"

"I don't think Dean would have murdered them," she declared on a grimace. "They were very close."

"Or they *were* very close, until your father put him behind bars."

She sucked in her breath at that. "Good point. So you think Dean could be the one sending me emails and leaving behind animal carcasses? I don't see that. And why would Dean come after me now?"

"I don't know," Declan admitted, as he looked down at the War Dog. "Honestly Shelby's arrival could have triggered it."

"No, that doesn't make any sense because I was getting those threatening letters before."

He nodded. "True, and maybe that's all it was. Maybe

somebody—whether Dean or someone else—just got irritated that you were around and didn't like the fact that you were living the life of the innocent, when he had suffered so much."

She winced. "And that makes me sound even worse in Dean's eyes or whoever's doing all this. No way I can make Dean's years lost in prison now somehow good. If he was truly innocent, he's understandably angry." She sagged down onto the couch beside Declan. "I would really hate to think that he was innocent and was put away because of my parents."

"Well, regardless of how you feel about it, that part might end up getting fixed. Dean's opened an inquiry to have his case reexamined."

Her jaw dropped. "Oh my God." She shook her head frantically. "But …" Then she quieted.

"But then what?"

"That doesn't sound like a guilty man," she declared. "A guilty man would just take his freedom and run."

"Yes, a lot of men would, but, in this case, if Dean firmly believes that he's innocent and that potentially he was set up, … he'll try to reopen the case to get down to the truth. As long as he is deemed guilty, nobody will look at anything else."

"Jesus, that's the last thing I want to go through."

"Will it have anything to do with you?" Declan asked curiously.

She frowned at him. "I don't know. Is it possible? I cannot be involved in that too."

"I don't know," Declan admitted, "but I would think that, as part of that investigation, you would at the least have some investigators coming here to talk to you."

"And again I don't know anything about it," she declared.

"And yet we have this person in your life who's potentially causing you trouble."

"Yeah, but I don't know who it is or why they're trying to cause trouble. Even if it's Dean, I didn't have anything to do with his incarceration or his court-martial. So the whole thing just feels wrong."

"And it's possible that it is just wrong," Declan noted. "So, no matter what it is, let's get to the bottom of it."

She nodded slowly. "If you think that's what I should do."

"More to the point, what do you want to do? Do you want to get to the bottom of this? Do you want to see this man?"

"I actually enjoyed spending time with him years ago," she shared, "but it's been a long time."

"For him too," Declan added. "Any idea why he was around your family so much?"

She shrugged. "I don't know. He's a vague memory, but I do remember lots of happy times where he was included. But it's like this faded image of when I was a child, like five or six, that type of thing. Twenty years later is a long time." She stared out into the living room. "And you saw a younger man leaving here, right?"

"Yes, he was," Declan confirmed. "And you're right. I don't think it would have been Dean, but that doesn't mean it wasn't somebody he hired, somebody who he knows, or somebody who suffered because he was in jail. Did he have a family?"

She shook her head. "None that I ever knew of, but I'm sure you guys have access to that information more than I do."

He brought up his phone, checked the file, and shook his head. "I don't see any relatives listed here, not living at this point."

"I think he was kind of sweet on my mom," Carly said softly, thinking back over the years, "but obviously I don't really have anything specific to say about it."

"Then let's go meet him," Declan suggested, "and, that way, even if you do have to talk to the authorities about it, you'll have a more current reference in your mind. And don't worry. I'll be there to ensure you're protected, just in case you're feeling threatened in any way."

"Just the idea of going makes me feel threatened," she admitted, struggling visibly in front of him.

"I'm sorry, but whatever it is that's going on in your world seems to have brought something out into the open."

"Yet there was no need for it. There was no need for any of this to come out in the open."

"Well, that depends on what *out in the open* means to you," Declan pointed out, with a smile. "If you think about it, and if Dean is looking for vindication and to get his honor back, not to mention the practical matter of his pension, then I guess, from my perspective, I would like to see where it goes."

"Right." She frowned. "And none of this means my parents were somehow involved. It just means that they were convinced that Dean was."

"Exactly. And sometimes we get convinced of the wrong thing because of other people."

She nodded slowly. "Fine." She got up and abruptly walked out of the room.

Declan picked up the phone and called the number that

Badger had given him. When a tired-sounding older man answered, Declan explained who he was and that he wanted to come talk to him.

First came silence on the other end. "Does she want to come?" he asked for the second time.

"She would like to meet with you, yes. She's not sure what happened. She understands that you're trying to open up the case to clear your name, so, of course, she's worried that it would impact her world, but she would also like to get to the truth."

"Well, it would be nice if somebody in that family did," he replied, his voice weary. "I never did anything to hurt them."

"Look. I didn't know these people, and I don't know to what extent their own sense of honor might have gotten in the way or whether they trusted somebody else, and maybe that's all it was."

"I don't know either," Dean replied, "but I would definitely like to have some closure myself."

"Of course you would. When can we come talk to you?"

"Better do it now," Dean stated, "before I lose my nerve. Twenty years is a long time."

"It is, indeed. She's a little worried that you'll be aggressive or angry and take it out on her."

"No, never," Dean claimed. "She was the cutest little thing. And I look back on all the years that I missed of her growing up, and it's just … hard," he admitted.

"Fine, I'll talk to her, and we will be there as soon as we can." With that, Declan hung up and walked into the kitchen. Carly stood there, her arms crossed over her chest, staring out the window. "Well, Dean would like very much to see you."

She jolted. And then she slowly nodded. "I guess that's the least I can do, isn't it?"

"He would like you to keep an open mind, and he hopes that we can come up with some kind of an understanding as to what happened."

"You told him that I don't know anything, right?"

"Yeah, I sure did. Though, from his perspective, that may or may not be true. We don't always know what it is that we actually know. I think it's better that we go now."

She nodded. "Yeah, before I lose my nerve."

"Funny, that's exactly what he told me."

She looked startled for a moment and then nodded. "*Ugh*, let's go figure this out." She looked at the dogs and back at him.

He whistled for Shelby. "Pick one of the others too," he said.

She smiled and called Madge. Madge and Shelby came, and they quickly leashed them up. So, with the two dogs in tow, they headed out to his vehicle. She asked Declan, "Do you know where Dean lives?"

Declan nodded. "I'll punch it into the GPS. We shouldn't be too long. It's not too far away."

"I thought you mentioned earlier it was like three hours away."

"That was per the data Badger sent me. However, Dean gave me a different address than the one on file, so it's closer."

She shrugged and didn't say much. As they got closer, she muttered, "This is really unnerving."

"I know," Declan acknowledged, "and for a lot of different reasons. You're worried that it would impact your memory of your parents. And you're also worried that maybe they were wrong and that maybe an innocent man was court-martialed and imprisoned on their say-so."

She nodded. "How can I not be worried about that? I mean, my parents were good people, but, like everyone, they were human and not infallible."

"Nope, nobody is."

They pulled up in front of a small older home, not dilapidated but definitely in need of care. Declan parked at the curb, double-checked the address, and nodded. "This is it."

"Okay, here goes nothing."

"If it gets ugly, we can always leave," he told her immediately.

"Right. ... I guess it depends on what you mean by *ugly*."

He smiled. "Hey, I'm here on your side, you know?"

"Yet, at the same time, we want to get to the bottom of it, so I can't be too much of a baby over the whole thing," she admitted. She got out of the vehicle and brought out the dogs, making sure that they were behaving at her side, and then walked slowly to the front door. It opened before they got there.

A man who she didn't recognize at all stepped out. Older, stooped, and definitely not in the best of health, he walked down the sidewalk toward her. "Hello, Carly. I would have recognized you anywhere."

She gave him a sad smile. "I can't say the same for you."

"No, I guess not," he replied, still giving her a smile. "The years haven't been easy on me."

"I'm so sorry. I don't even know when it all happened, much less what, but the fact that you're doing even as well as you are speaks volumes."

"I don't know," Dean disagreed. "Sometimes I think I'm

lucky to be alive at all."

"I imagine that is a sentiment many people would agree with."

He shook her hand and then shook Declan's. "I find it interesting that you guys contacted me," Dean noted. "I've been in touch with the military about opening my case."

"I am more than happy to help in any way I can," Carly replied. "I just honestly don't know very much. My parents would never talk about it."

He nodded. "They were my best friends, you know? … And I was happily in love with your mother."

She chuckled. "I do remember hearing a little bit about that," she quipped, with a fond smile.

He nodded. "It wasn't anything I ever tried to hide, but obviously it wasn't something I got in their faces about either." Dean chuckled. "She was a beautiful woman, and I'm so sorry that she's gone."

"Do you know what happened?" she asked him.

"To your parents? No, I just heard that they were both deceased." He looked puzzled. "Why do you ask?"

She looked over at Declan. "I don't know what to say," she muttered.

"Why don't we try the truth and set the tone for the day," Declan suggested.

She frowned at him. "Well, that's what I was hoping for." Looking over at the old man, she shared, "Both of my parents were murdered."

He stared at her in shock, his jaw dropping. "What? No!"

She nodded. "About six years ago."

"Unfortunately for you," Declan added, "they were murdered at the same time you were released for your father's funeral."

The old man looked like he'd taken a second visible blow. "No," he cried out, "no, that's not possible."

"Well, that's part of what we're trying to get to the bottom of because …" Declan looked around. "Is there any chance we could take this inside?"

"Of course." Dean motioned back to the house. "Come on in. Bring the dogs too." As they got closer, he said, "It's not much though." He looked over at her. "I haven't really had a chance to get my life together yet. This house belonged to my parents."

"I'm sorry about that, the turn in your life." She pointed at the house. "Still, it's a home."

"Well, it is now," he agreed, with a smile. He led the way inside, where quite a bit of ancient furniture remained. In the living room, he motioned to the chairs. "Please sit down. I must say, I'm still in shock over your news. I thought maybe my news about reopening the case would be the shocker of the day, but it appears to be yours instead."

"Well, I'm not looking to one-up you on anything," she muttered, "particularly with something like that."

"No, no, of course not. That was crass of me. I'm sorry."

She smiled. "Hey, I just want to get to the bottom of all this."

"Oh, I understand that your interest in this and mine are two different things," Dean admitted, with half a smile. "But, in the end, it seems we may have some information to exchange here. I didn't know about your parents." He shook his head, looking bewildered. "In fact, I had been sitting here, trying to convince myself that I could contact them and ask for their help. Then I found out from another friend in the military that they were gone—but he sure didn't say anything about murder."

"I'm surprised," Declan replied, "more about that than anything else."

"It seems odd he didn't mention the murder part," Carly added, "since it was all over the news."

"Of course it was. Bad news always travels that way." Dean nodded. "Then I didn't ask for any details. I never asked about your mother at all." He frowned. "Both of them?"

She nodded. "Both of them."

"Dear God. I'm so sorry, Carly. That must have been terrible for you."

"It was quite an ugly time, yes."

At that point, Declan looked over at Dean. "Unfortunately her troubles aren't over either."

The old man looked at him in surprise. "What do you mean?"

"She's been getting threatening emails and even intruders into her place," Declan explained. "We're trying to figure out if any of this is connected."

The old man just stared at him, bewildered. "Good Lord." He shook his head wearily. "Hasn't she been through enough?"

"If I have any say in the matter, the answer is yes. Declan here is wondering if it's connected to her." Carly raised the leash on Shelby, who now rested on the floor, looking at Dean. Shelby wasn't growling, but she wasn't relaxed either. "Shelby here is a War Dog, and we're wondering if any of this has anything to do with the fact that she just came into my possession."

He stared at the War Dog, and it was obvious that he was struggling to connect all the dots. "Why on earth would having a War Dog be related in any way to my court-martial?"

"That's what we don't know," she replied.

Dean shook his head, sat here for a moment, obvious that he was trying to absorb all the information. "Good Lord. You know, when you go into prison, access to information is limited. The mainstream news of the world is available of course, and I kept abreast of a lot of it. At some point in time, some of that anger and sense of injustice faded, and I just got tired. When I was released, I wanted to come out and lead a peaceful, happy life. I don't imagine I have too many years left. Doing time like that isn't easy, and I'm that much older now," he stated. "You don't ever forget, but, at the same time, I really don't want to focus on what I went through. I just wanted to come out, try to make amends with my friends, reassure them that I truly was innocent, and move on from there."

Declan wondered if it were really possible to have that sense of peacefulness over it all. "Have you really forgiven them for their part in it all?"

Dean looked at Declan in surprise and then nodded. "The thing about them," he shared, with a wry tone, "is that they were absolutely sincere. Agree or not, I knew that they believed what they thought they had on me, and it killed them to go to court against me. Yet they firmly believed that I'd done what they accused me of doing, and there didn't seem to be anything I could do to tell them otherwise."

"How do you feel now?"

"For the longest time I was terribly hurt and so angry—because we were the best of friends. There was absolutely no reason for them to have believed anybody telling them tales about me. I mean, seriously no reason. Yet ..."

"Yet?"

"Yet in time," Dean related, "they obviously came to believe somebody, and I think that hurt me the most. And, if you think I had anything to do with the charges, please don't think that," he stated immediately. "I've spent many years confused and trying to straighten things out, and it's exhausting. I wasn't planning to do this much, but I just don't want to die as a convicted traitor to my country. And stealing? ... That is not something I could ever do. I really don't want my legacy to be that of a traitorous thief. I don't know who or what has gone wrong in both of our worlds"—he waved his hand—"but it's a bit of a stretch for me to think that our problems could be related. However, if we could manage to solve one, I would truly be grateful if we could then solve the other."

And, with that, Dean fell silent, but not before Declan caught sight of a sheen of tears in his eyes.

CHAPTER 4

CARLY WAS SILENT most of the drive home. When they were a couple blocks away, she said, "There's a coffee shop in the park up ahead."

Declan nodded and immediately detoured and pulled into the drive-through. "Is the park at a lake?"

She laughed. "Yes, it is, and, man, I could use some time there today."

He followed her directions, pulled into a parking lot, and, with the two dogs more than eager to get out and to jump around, he led the way. Once they got down to the dock area, he asked, "Do you want to let them go?"

"Well, I don't know about Shelby," she replied, looking at Declan in surprise.

"She'll be fine," he stated. "I know how to call her back." When he reached out a hand for Shelby's leash, Carly gave it to him automatically. He unclipped Shelby and told her to go swim. Shelby took one look at him, and then, with unfettered joy, she raced toward the lake and dove in.

It was all Carly could do to not cry when she saw the absolute joy as the dog jumped and sprawled through the water, coming up for air, then going back under again, over and over. "How did you know?" she asked.

"I saw her reaction as we drove up closer to the water." He chuckled. "If ever a dog wanted in that water, it was

Shelby." He looked down at Madge. "What about her?"

"Oh, heavens no, she's too much of a lady," Carly said on a laugh, looking down at Madge, who stared in disdain at the antics of the other dog.

"It's really good for Shelby to be in a normal household," Declan noted.

She looked at him hopefully. "Have you talked to your bosses about that yet?"

"About you and Shelby? A little." He nodded. "Honestly there just hasn't been time for any more than a quick conversation."

She winced. "I know. There's just been so much chaos."

"So, what did you think about what Dean had to say?" Declan asked her, as they walked along the dock.

"I believed him." She stepped up to Declan's side. "Of course, nothing like a few tears to make that happen. I just …" She got lost in her thoughts, as she looked up ahead. "I don't think the tears were forced or anything, but I still think Dean's gotten a raw deal somehow. I think it broke his heart that my parents believed whatever they were told."

"And that's another thing. Do you think they had any ax to grind over this?"

"I hope not," she declared, making no attempt to defend, delay, or deliberately misunderstand what he was saying. "I would like to think that my parents were solid, but obviously something like this brings up a lot of questions."

"Well, one issue is where would they have found out about the theft, and why would they have gone to court against him?"

"They were very moral people," she stated. "There was never any doubt in their minds what was right and what was wrong. If they had any inkling that something was not quite right, then I could see them doing something like this. But really, when you look at it closely, the whole thing just seems so very far-fetched."

"I get it. It's also a heartbreaker to think that they may have been wrong."

"More than a heartbreaker," she said. "It would devastate me to think that somebody suffered so terribly because of how strongly they believed in something that they weren't right about."

He nodded. "The thing is, we can't blame them because we can't even ask them any questions. Did they leave any notes, journals, or anything of that nature behind?"

She shrugged. "If they did, I don't know that I would have known about it," she said. "There was plenty going on at that time in our lives, but I know they were trying to be stoic and to just get through the process. But again, I was kept out of a lot of it, and much of it happened when they were out of the house. They were gone for days at a time. She'd come back, then he would go again and that sort of thing. There were periods of complete sadness, I guess, though that may not be the right word. But I remember not long afterward, when I asked them about their friend, being told that he wouldn't be coming anymore. I didn't get a whole lot about it until much later, maybe when I was teenager, and then they told me that he'd been convicted of theft. They sounded very sad about the whole thing, as if they couldn't quite believe it themselves."

"And given what we now know, maybe they didn't. Maybe they were holding out hope that it would be found and proven that he wasn't guilty."

"Maybe. That would be a nice thing to think, but is it true? I don't know." And she didn't know. Not at all. It was impossible to figure it out at this point either. "I mean, if Dean's telling the truth, I would very much like to have his name cleared and to have the guilty party caught." Breaking eye contact, she asked Declan a question. "Just before we left, you asked him for something in an email. I didn't hear it though, so what was that about?"

"I asked him for a list of anyone who might be upset that he was charged and convicted of something like this, as well as who he had seen when he was out those few years ago at the funeral. He didn't like me asking, and, of course, all of his friends and his parents, who died a while back, have been torn over all this as well. But, in order to come to the bottom of it, we have to know."

"Right. I guess it could be somebody in his world, couldn't it?"

"Or it could also be the person who's guilty of the very crime he paid the price for."

She looked at Declan, clearly startled. "Wouldn't that be something? But why kill my parents?"

"Maybe so the truth behind it could never be found. Maybe the witness was paid to lie. Maybe your parents were paid to lie." He glanced at her and looked away quickly. "Maybe they were blackmailed. Maybe it had nothing to do with your parents at all, just that their killer may have been afraid they would back out or something after the fact. Who knows really. There are too many possibilities."

"Maybe my parents found out the truth," she murmured, immediately twisting around.

He looked at her in surprise and nodded. "That makes sense too."

"And it's the answer I would prefer, of course," she noted, with a little smile.

"None of us ever want to think of our family being involved in something nefarious, and don't worry. I'm not saying they were," he added immediately. "I'm just saying that what we really need to do is find some answers."

"Yeah, well, I'm not exactly sure how to do that. And obviously Dean's court-martial would be completely unrelated to what's going on in my world now."

He frowned at her. "Do you think so?"

Startled, she glanced at him. "Why would it be related?"

"I don't know," he admitted. "Your parents, do you have any of their belongings still?"

"Sure," she said. "What I kept is stored upstairs in the attic." Then her color faded. "Jesus, do you think that's what the intruder was all about? He took an awful chance being in my home in broad daylight."

"I think that means he saw that you were in the backyard," Declan clarified. "Maybe he knew what you were doing and that you would be there for an hour or so, so he would pop up in your attic and take a look. Maybe he figured he could be up there quietly for as long as he needed to be—or even stay up there."

She sucked in her breath, staring at him in shock.

"Not that I want to bring up that possibility, but—"

"You just did, which scares the crap out of me."

"That's only because of all the TV and movie horror shows, and the books they are based on, about strangers living in fake rooms or attics, while the rest of the family sleeps in blissful innocence," he explained. "I can't tell you what this guy was doing, but we definitely need to find out."

"Do you have any idea how to do that?"

"I've been tossing around a few ideas. I'm not sure I have the solution quite yet, but it will help when we get that list from Dean."

"But that won't necessarily tell us anything in particular about who was at my place."

"Maybe not, but it might give us a lead."

"Not if Dean's the guilty party."

"And that's why I want to see whatever you have that was left by your parents."

"Okay. I can show you when we get back home. And, after what you just said, we'll have to go up and confirm nobody's moved in up there anyway."

"That's a good idea too."

They watched as Shelby raced around in the water and now onto the shore, coming back toward them and showering them with freezing cold water, before ducking off again.

"Good thing we're in your vehicle," she noted ruefully, "because that dog will bring back a ton of water with her."

"Yep, but look at her demeanor. See how happy she is?"

Carly chuckled. "Hard to believe you're not a dog owner."

"Are you kidding?"

"Okay, you got me there," she replied. "But, if you're a dog owner, you're also a house owner, so what else is going on in your life? I'm surprised you can just drop everything and stay here for a few days."

"That's because I don't have a house. And, while I always had a dog or two of my own before my time in the military, plus plenty of War Dog contact while in the service, now I just dog sit as needed for friends, until I can get set up in a proper home with a yard for several dogs. I don't actually have very much at all right now," he shared. "In fact, I recently moved to an apartment in Oregon, about three hours from here, to help out an old buddy. He's ex-military too. I had figured we would toss around some ideas for the rest of our lives, but instead I added on ramps to his house. Before that I helped out Badger, so I just rented a set of rooms close to where he lives in New Mexico because I was doing a lot of work for them back then, since they had taken on a bunch of building projects for other injured vets. Things like, getting them set up in houses and making things wheelchair accessible, plus a few other things along that line," he told her. "Then I had to go back in for some additional surgery. So I had to recover for a bit. Therefore, for now, I'm dogless. It suits me to not have much in the way of luggage, as I determine my next path in life."

"Luggage and baggage," she added, with a nod.

"Exactly." He smiled. "See? You do understand."

"Footloose, fancy-free, and figuring out where you want to go next."

"True." He nodded, eyeing her with admiration. "You got that all sorted out, didn't you? I was actually worried you might decide I was homeless, jobless, and looking for a place to crash for a few days, and, as such, here taking advantage of you."

At that, she burst out laughing. "I don't see you as someone who takes advantage." She still giggled at the thought. "I mean, I can see you giving someone the shirt off your back, but I really don't see you as the type who would move in and not move out."

"That's a real thing, you know? There have been all kinds of problems with people pulling that squatter's crap like that," he noted, shaking his head.

"That's because the world is full of other people, so it's up to us to ensure our world is the way we want it."

At that, Shelby raced over once more and collapsed at

their feet, her tail still wagging joyfully.

"Now that is one happy dog," Carly noted, as she crouched beside the War Dog and rubbed her belly. "This is really good for her, isn't it?"

"It really is," he confirmed. "Any kind of stress relief, especially considering the upset from the last few days. She's also dealing with strangers and vehicles, so anything that helps her to settle in is a good thing."

Carly gave the dog another cuddle. "As much as I'd love to stay here at the park with the dogs, you've now got me thinking about my attic."

"Good. Let's go." And, with that, he led the way back to his vehicle in the parking lot.

Before she got in, she stopped. "This may sound strange," she said, looking over the roof of his vehicle, "but do you feel like we're being followed?"

He nodded. "Yes, in fact a car pulled into the park not long after we did. I don't know whether I should feel happy or sad that you noticed."

She stared at him. "Are we in danger?"

"I can't answer that yet. However, believe me. As soon as I do, I'll let you know. Now let's get in and get going."

"But I don't want to lead this asshole right to my house."

"We won't." Declan gave her a feral grin. "We'll take him for a ride, and, if we're lucky, we might get some information from him."

"Like?"

"Hopefully the make of his vehicle and the license plate number."

"What will that tell us? I mean, it might give us a name, but it won't give us much else, will it?"

"Oh, it could give us more," he replied, "but I suspect that, if they have gotten away with everything they have done so far, the car will probably be stolen." And, with that, he got into the driver's side and closed the door hard.

Declan pulled out of the parking lot, checking to see if they were being followed. Soon after hitting the main highway, he abruptly pulled off to the side and made it look like he was on the phone, so the vehicle coming up behind them didn't have any choice but to drive on by. He opened the window, hoping to get a look at the driver, who looked right, then hesitated, and, lacking much choice, kept on going.

"Oh my gosh, that was a smooth maneuver," Carly noted.

Declan shrugged. "It's a pretty easy one."

"I guess I'll have to remember that," she murmured.

"Hopefully, after this, you won't ever come up against something like it again." He flashed that trademark grin of his at her.

"Still, it was quite smart and ever so simple. You didn't really give them a choice."

"My granddad had this to say about horses, and it applies to people as well. You make the right choice easy and the wrong choice difficult." His grandfather had spent more than a few hours on the back of cranky horses, training them. But it was simple advice that Declan had stuck by, and it made sense to him. It was one of those useful tips about life.

It really applied to everything, from partnerships to raising kids. Make the right thing easy and the wrong thing difficult. He could see that Carly was still mulling it over in her head. "Shall we make a stop to pick up some groceries?" he asked.

She stared at him, startled. "I haven't been into my own fridge in a couple days, so I'm not sure. You're probably in a better position to answer that question than I am."

At that, he took a quick detour to a supermarket. As he parked out front, he asked, "Do you want to stay here with the dogs?"

She nodded. "I am feeling a bit tired."

"Good enough. I'll just dash in. Keep the doors locked." Startled, she looked at him. He shrugged. "We don't know where he is, but you can bet he didn't go far."

"Crap, maybe I'm not too tired after all," she stated, "but I can't leave the animals here."

"No, and we're in a public place, so you'll be just fine. You've got Shelby, plus I'll keep an eye on you from the window."

"Do that, please, and hurry."

He dashed into the grocery store, snagged a shopping cart, and grabbed stuff for burgers, plus eggs, bacon, sandwich meat, bread, a variety of fresh vegetables, and a couple steaks. He figured they could always come back in a day or two as well. By the time he got through the check stand and back out again, he saw with relief that she was still just sitting there. As he walked closer, another vehicle ripped in front of him, forcing him to step back. It was actually close enough that he had to wonder, and suddenly she was there beside him.

"Are you okay?" she asked.

He nodded. "Yeah. Did you get a look at the vehicle?"

She nodded. "I think it was him."

"I do too, which means he's getting mighty pissed." He put the groceries in his vehicle, and, with the dogs barking like crazy, got in and drove out in the same direction the other vehicle took.

"You're not going after him, are you?" She gasped.

"What do you want me to do? Wait around for him to try again?" He tried to keep his tone calm and thought about it for a moment. To him it was a reasonable thing to head out after this guy, but he could tell from her reaction that she wasn't happy about it at all.

"Oh fine, he's probably too far ahead anyway." So, with that, he drove to her house, circling the block first. When he pulled up in front of the driveway, he kept a close eye all the way around. "I didn't see him on the way back, so hopefully we're all clear for the moment."

She nodded and slowly got out of the vehicle. "I don't know about you, but this is an awful lot of excitement."

He smiled. "I know, but it'll calm right down, as soon as we get to the bottom of it."

"So why do I feel like there's a storm to come first?"

"Because there is, no two ways about it."

"*Great*, but thank you for being honest with me."

"Hey, we'll keep our heads about us and stay the course." Declan quickly texted Badger, asking if he had gotten a return on the license plate he's texted him. Badger called as Declan was putting the groceries away. "Hey," he answered. "Anything?"

"Stolen."

"That's what I figured and says an awful lot."

"Sure it does. This guy has gone to a lot of trouble to hide something."

"The question is, what is it he's trying to hide?"

"Exactly," Badger replied.

"We'll go up and take a look in the attic as soon as I get the groceries put away," Declan shared. "She's got some things that belonged to her parents up there. I'll go take a look at them and see what is there. I also wonder if maybe the intruder that I saw here that day had been upstairs."

"Would she have known?"

"She was outside at the time," Declan said, "and, from the looks of it, the attic is pretty easily accessed without making too much noise."

"Keep me apprised." With that, Badger hung up.

Finished with the groceries, Declan turned to face her. "Let's go."

She was still staring at him, half numb. "That's fine, unless you want me to put more coffee on." He eyed the pot, considering. She shook her head. "No, I'd rather go up and deal with this now."

"What do you think we'll find?"

"I have no idea," she murmured. "I wouldn't have thought there was anything to find. I just brought with me what was left after I got their place cleaned up."

"How much did you get rid of?"

"Most of it," she said. "There were sentimental things, but I couldn't stay in the house and didn't have money to pay for long-term storage. So, I kept the things that were important to me and some of the family legacy-type stuff, and that was it."

"Good, so we won't have too much to go through then."

But as they got upstairs, she gasped. "This is not how I left it."

He surveyed the room and nodded. "So, this is what the

guy was after."

"I don't know what he was after or what he thought he would find, but does this mess mean he found it or not?"

"I'm not sure, but it looks like he got a little pissed off in the process."

"You think?" she quipped in a fury. "And I didn't even know. Do you think he came up more than once?"

"I don't know, but I did see him that day. He didn't have anything with him, unless it was chucked into a pocket or under his clothes. I didn't see anything beyond that."

"Right." She took a deep breath. "Well, at least straightening up the mess he made will help me sort what's here."

"Do you need to sort what's here?"

"I don't know, but I'm starting to feel like he came here looking for something specific. I just don't know what it might be."

"Okay, so that's what we'll find out. Let's get some boxes and start repacking this stuff."

"Actually, while we're at it, I wouldn't mind maybe taking a closer look, and, if I can get rid of some of this, then maybe I should." When he looked at her sharply, she shrugged. "You can only hang on to stuff for so long, and then it just becomes more weight on my shoulders."

"Oh, I agree with you completely. So, if you're ready to let more of it go, let's do it."

She smiled. "Thank you. Not only for cheering me on, but just ... thanks so much for sticking around."

He shook his head. "Hey, no way you're getting rid of me now." He brushed the tears from her cheek with his thumb. "And you're safe, I promise."

She nodded. "You know? For the first time in a very long while, I can see this coming to an end. In a way, it feels like all I've done up until now is run."

"Because you have, and that's the thing about a prosthetic."

She looked at him in surprise. "What?"

"I don't run worth a damn anymore." He chuckled. "So rather than do a half-ass job of running, I'd much rather stop, turn around, and take the fight right back to them."

She burst out laughing at that, then the two of them sat down and got to work.

CHAPTER 5

SHE HAD BEEN choking back hidden tears, as they studied the attic. At least she had hoped they were hidden, until he ran a hand along her cheek. Now that hand was on her shoulder.

"I know it's hard," Declan said. "We've just ripped open a painful part of your family life again, but that sense of a violation, knowing that asshole was up here, is a big deal, and you're right to be upset."

She nodded immediately. "I was just thinking that, trying not to get too emotional about it, but, at the same time, it is a terrible violation."

He nodded. "Of course it is, and that's another reason we need to make this stop for good."

"I wish." She then pointed at some random paperwork on the floor. Evidence her visitor had, indeed, been here. "I don't even know what he was looking for."

Declan bent down and picked up the files in front of him. "*Huh*, these are on the court-martial case."

"So why didn't he take that, if that was what he was after?"

"Maybe he sat here and read it but didn't find what he was looking for. Is there any more that was theirs?"

"I think we could go through all this and not find any useful, just like my intruder did."

Declan shrugged. "We won't know that until we look through all this. I know it may take a while, but let's speed-read these docs and see if anything jumps out at us." She nodded, and they dug in.

A couple hours later, she rubbed the back of her head. "I'm getting a headache from the dust."

"No small wonder," he murmured. "If there is anything else, maybe we should take it downstairs."

She looked at him in surprise and nodded. "We probably should have done that from the beginning honestly."

"We still can, and a bunch of these files I actually want to go through more carefully."

"It's not as if we can do much to make a difference now."

"I don't know about that." He gave her a smirk. "Do you see anything else that might be useful?"

She stood, moved a few boxes that they had repacked, and turned around full circle. "Oh, an envelope is back here." She bent down and grabbed it. "It's a black file folder actually. It was hard to see."

Declan instantly held out his hand.

She looked at him in surprise, yet handed it over. "What makes you so happy to see this one?"

"Well, if we didn't see it, chances are your intruder didn't either."

She felt some excitement building inside. "I didn't even think of that." She squatted beside Declan to check it out.

Declan groaned. "It's too hard to read up here. Let's take all this down, and, if we need to, we can come back up here later."

"Good enough. At least if he was here and didn't see anything—"

"Exactly. If he realized there isn't anything here to find, he won't come back."

"And yet you don't sound happy about that."

"Personally I hope he does come back. My fist would like to have a chat with him."

She snorted at that. "I don't know if they just make them cocky in the navy or what," she said, "but that prosthetic doesn't make you the best fighter anymore." He froze, looked at her, and she immediately backed up. "*Uh-oh*, I gather it's a touchy subject. Sorry."

"I might have a prosthetic, but trust me. It doesn't make me any less of a fighter."

She held up her hands, stepping back once more. "I didn't mean to imply that."

He nodded. "Yeah, you did. I'm just telling you that you're wrong. And you don't ever need to back up from me like that. I would never hurt you." And, with that, he stormed downstairs.

It was her fault because she had more or less implied that he shouldn't be trying to fight at all, and that came off as a judgment on her part. As she walked into the kitchen, he was putting on coffee. "Declan, I'm sorry. I wasn't thinking."

He just shrugged.

"I am so sorry. I didn't mean that you aren't capable. And I understand. I'm sure you've already heard that a time or two already. You didn't need to hear it from me as well. I wish I could take it back. Truly."

"People automatically decide that I'm somehow less than I was after they find out about the prosthetic," he explained, "but they're wrong." His tone was hard, yet his voice was a bit too calm and controlled.

She realized he wasn't angry so much as just … this was

something that he'd heard enough times that he didn't want to hear it anymore.

"Did you ever do any self-defense work afterward?"

He snorted. "I didn't need to do self-defense work. Believe me. The kind of work that I did beforehand was something I went right back into training for."

"Did you think you could get back into doing the same kind of work?"

"No, but I also knew that physical fitness would be the answer, so I needed to be in prime condition in order to find something out there for me. Right up to the day I left, I was training, and I probably always will be. It's just really important to me."

She didn't say anything at first, just studied him, kicking herself for her heartless comment. She knew further apologies would not lessen the hurt she had caused. "I took some self-defense classes, ... after my parents were murdered. I probably should have kept it up, but I didn't. Part of that whole denial thing again."

"People tend to go both ways," he replied. "Some go one way, while the others go the opposite. Either making the most of it or getting hung up on it and becoming paranoid."

"Do they?"

"I was paranoid for a long time," he admitted, now facing her. "I didn't want it to affect me long-term like that, but it's hard to stop. It became something I had to intentionally work on."

"For the longest time I didn't even want to leave the house because I was sure somebody was out there who would get me."

"And maybe there was," he said. "Until we get to the bottom of this, I have no idea whether you might have been next on this hit list or not."

"Well, if I was, they gave up pretty damn fast."

"And that could just as easily be because Dean was convicted. Maybe if he hadn't been, it would have been a different story."

"So, you're saying that because Dean took the fall, the other guy was safe? And now that Dean is out and my parents are gone, the fact that Dean is reopening the investigation puts the real thief at risk again. That does make sense, doesn't it?"

"It does, which is also why your intruder's looking to make sure there is no evidence. If Dean reopened the case, our intruder is probably thinking there might be something here. It's possible he might have missed something, and now he's just crossing his *T*s and dotting his *I*s to confirm."

"And yet you mentioned my intruder was young."

Declan nodded. "I also didn't get a great look at him, so believe me. I've been questioning myself on that too."

"That's just part and parcel, isn't it?"

"It sure is." He gave her a small smile.

She hoped he was beginning to forgive her. Regardless she was happy to see that, when he got mad, he remained in control, his reason ruling, not his emotions. Which was a relief, considering how big he was and how little she was. Plus he told her why he reacted that way. She would never underestimate him again. She felt so bad for hurting him. She may never forgive herself. At least now he was looking at her and seemed to be back to his unprovoked self.

"Now that we have coffee, let's take this into the living room and see what's up." With that, he handed her a cup of coffee and then picked up his cup, grabbed the black file, and headed into the other room.

She followed along behind him. "I also need to get back to my work here," she noted. "I've had a couple days off, but that doesn't make the lives of my patients any easier."

"Can you take the rest of today off, then start back again tomorrow?"

She nodded. "That's exactly what I was thinking. I contacted the hospital and canceled the one session I was supposed to do today. They understood, but some of the patients will struggle. They really look forward to these days. Then tomorrow I don't have anything. However, I could double up our visits on the following day."

"Of course. So we'll get out and around everywhere that we need to get to. Just tell me when."

She smiled. "That almost sounds like you think you'll drive me around," she teased. "Did I just inherit a chauffeur as well?" His grin flashed, making her heart stumble.

"Maybe," he hedged. "Like I told you before, you won't get rid of me that easy, and, after being followed today, we're not taking any chances." With that, he brushed past her and walked into the living room, where he sat down in the big easy chair.

With her coffee in hand, she headed in and sat down on the chair beside him. "Do you really think he was trying to follow us? Even to the grocery store?"

"No doubt. He may follow our every move, just to see if we lead him to what he wants," Declan agreed cheerfully. "But the fact that he's done what he did—swerving his vehicle my way—tells us that we're on the right track. I couldn't be happier."

She shook her head. "You know that doesn't make much sense."

"It makes a ton of sense. You're just seeing it from a victim's point of view. I'm looking at it as a hunter. Up until now, we've only wondered if this was happening, but now that he's following us and trying to run us down, we know that we're pushing the right buttons. Now we just need to keep pushing until something breaks."

"As long as it's not you or me," she exclaimed. "I've already seen the ugliness that goes along with something breaking."

He nodded. "That's also why we have to make sure that, once it breaks this time, it doesn't break ever again. It needs to come to an end. Then you can move on with your life, and so can Dean."

"What about you?" she asked, studying him.

He flashed her that wonderful smile again. "Me too. Now if only I knew what, where, and how."

DECLAN LIT THE barbecue and tossed on the burgers. He thought about his words—what, where, and how—while he cooked. It was easy to say but harder to do. He had no idea what he would do after this. No idea where he wanted to go.

He liked being here and enjoyed being with Carly very much. He absolutely loved Shelby and the other dogs, as they totally accepted him, no judgment whatsoever. He hated to admit it, but Carly's words from earlier had stung, and that was something he would have to work on. For so many people, especially those who didn't know him, it was an automatic and quite justifiable conclusion to come to. Yet to hear those same words from someone who supposedly *did* know him stung. It hurt a lot.

It didn't apply to him, even with the prosthetic. However, he really couldn't hold her responsible for such a logical thought process, but a layperson's thinking, not someone with more knowledge or personal experience. A lot of people did see an amputee as being less of a man. He would never see himself that way, but he'd already experienced enough prejudice from people that he kept himself to those who were more compatible with his own line of thinking.

Like Badger and his group, they were one of the best groups for Declan to hang with, to work with, to live nearby, and no way anybody would ever imply that they were less than in any way, shape, or form. Declan didn't want anybody to look at him that way either. He shrugged it off. He was willing to give her a pass.

Plus he still had this mess here to sort out, and that was a confusing issue all around. There didn't seem to be a rhyme or reason, yet he instinctively felt it was all connected somehow. Declan was still reserving judgment on Dean, though he appeared to have been treated poorly and suffered even, after being framed. At the same time, Declan couldn't quite be sure of Dean. It was still possible he was the one doing this to Carly on purpose, out of vengeance. Her problems could also be hers alone and completely unrelated to Dean or to her parents' murders.

While he stood here, thinking about it, his phone buzzed, and he looked down to see an email from Dean. Declan opened it to find an apology for it taking so long to provide the list. He read the email out loud.

"Sorry, this is all I could come up with. I still think you're barking up the wrong tree, but I'm doing my best to keep an open mind and to be helpful."

Below that was a list of four names. Declan immediately forwarded the email to Badger, hoping he might help run down the names."

Badger acknowledged with a thumbs-up, and that was it. Not that there was anything else to say, and Declan's time was better spent on the current tasks at hand.

Declan went back to barbecuing the burgers, and, by the time they were done, he stepped inside and called out, "Dinner's ready."

He found her sitting at the table on her phone. She smiled at him, ended her call, and said, "Hey, those look wonderful, and they smell even better."

He realized she already had everything prepped, with buns and all the fixings on the table. He put down the plate of burgers. "I can't remember the last time I had a barbecued hamburger."

She laughed. "I was just thinking the same thing. I don't know why I don't use the barbecue more often. Or ever, for that matter."

He nodded and smiled. "I think an awful lot of kitchen tools in the world are underutilized."

She shrugged. "No reason I shouldn't be barbecuing more though. I absolutely love the end result, but you know? Sometimes the process is more effort than it's worth. Especially just cooking for myself."

"I won't argue with you there. Coming out of rehab and being on my own, cooking was often more effort than I wanted to deal with."

"I'm hungry." She immediately picked up a burger, took a big bite, and immediately smiled at him.

"See?" he said. "Absolutely nothing like it."

"That flavor is amazing." She closed her eyes and just enjoyed it.

He watched, happy at her response. He tucked into his

own burger, and, by the time he thought to reach for a napkin to mop up his dripping hands, he was happily chewing through the last bite. "You're right. That really was fabulous." He immediately reached for a second, then looked over at her and asked, "Do you want another?"

She shook her head. "No way I could eat a second one," she protested. "I'm already stuffed."

He hesitated, and she shook her head. "No, you go ahead. I've never been able to eat more than one and have regretted it every time I've tried," she stated. "I would rather just remember how fabulous that was." She almost had an envious look in her gaze.

He quickly prepped the second one for himself, and, when he picked it up, she sighed.

"It does my heart good to see somebody eat properly."

He laughed at that. "Is there such a thing?'

"Well, sometimes you see people who just don't get it. Burgers are meant to be eaten just as they are, fresh and hot, which means they are a juicy mess." She shook her head. "Yet I know some people feel they need to take a knife and a fork to them because they couldn't possibly bite into them."

"Well, if you can't figure out a way to bite them"—he looked at her oddly—"a knife and fork won't help. It will just topple into pieces."

She grinned. "My folks were like that, especially my father. I did try to tell him that, but he was old school and always used a knife and a fork."

"I don't know. That might make me a little judgmental, but I don't think I could trust a man who wouldn't pick up a burger in his hands." At that, she went off in peals of laughter. He grinned at her. "It's good to hear you laugh. I haven't heard very much of it lately."

Immediately her humor died, and she nodded. "There hasn't been a whole lot to laugh about, you know?"

"And yet things are looking up," he reminded her.

She snorted. "Well, in some ways, yes, but it's not as if we have answers. I do appreciate you sticking around though."

He looked at her in surprise. "And here I was thinking that maybe you wanted me to leave, you know? Since I've been eating your food and all."

She laughed. "You mean, you're actually cooking all my food and serving me hot meals and looking after me. Not to mention being that voice of reason when things get a little scary."

He nodded. "Getting scary is kind of a normal thing when you get to this stage of chaos. That's why we need answers, and we need them as soon as possible."

"I don't suppose your friends came up with anything, did they?"

He shook his head. "I sent Badger all the names that Dean gave me. I think he sent you a copy of his email as well."

She nodded. "He did, and I took a look, but I didn't recognize any of the names."

"Good enough, though that wasn't unexpected."

"I was hoping I would see a name and immediately go, 'Aha, it's him,' you know?"

"Wow, wouldn't that be lovely. You do know that only happens in fiction and in the movies?"

She smiled, while shaking her head. "Not even in any of the movies I've seen lately, but I guess having Dean on board is a help."

Declan kept eating, and, when he was finally done, he

muttered, "That was fabulous."

"Well, you bought it, and you cooked it, but I will agree. It truly was fabulous."

He smiled at her. "Who bought it or cooked it doesn't matter to me. It was also the company."

She flashed him a bright smile. "That is actually something I haven't had a whole lot of lately."

"Too many bad memories?" he asked.

"No, not so much that." She frowned, then shrugged. "It's kind of hard to even figure out just what the problem is, but probably it's just that I don't trust that easily." Her voice grew quieter as she went on. "You know? After being so scared, having to deal with the trauma, and being alone on the property, I kind of went crazy with the dating for a time. But I didn't want to bring them home. I just wanted to know that I wasn't alone. When I realized what I was doing, I immediately stopped because I wasn't being fair to them. And now, as you can tell, I've still got some issues."

"I think you're doing remarkably well. We all have issues, but you're actually trying to do something about it," he pointed out, "so cut yourself some slack."

She laughed. "Yeah, well, that whole *cutting myself some slack* thing isn't really who I am."

"No, we're usually hardest on ourselves," Declan noted. "I get that. I do the same thing sometimes. The thing is, there's only so much we can do, and then we have to just let information filter toward us, or something has to come up so we can actually know what we're doing and how to change it. Right now, I need to know if any of those names have anything to do with this. It could give us a good lead if they do."

"Will it give us answers?"

"Not necessarily," he said. "We can only hope that they give us something to move forward on. Outside of this court-martial case that your parents were involved in, I can't really see who else could be involved. So I'm thinking it's most likely the person who actually did the stealing or a person looking for revenge."

She swallowed hard. "So you haven't taken Dean off the suspect list?"

Declan immediately shook his head. "No, I haven't, but do I think it's him? Not really, though I'm not sure. Do I believe he is completely off the hook in this? No, I can't say I feel that way either."

"Did he come across as credible?"

"Yes, absolutely," Declan declared.

"Is that enough to make me secure?"

Immediately he shook his head. "No, it sure isn't."

She let out a slow breath. "Good. I didn't want to make it sound as if I was being paranoid, but I didn't really feel comfortable enough to take him off my list either."

"We shouldn't take anybody off, not until we have a good idea what's going on. Even if it is Dean, there must be some connection between Dean and the young man who was here at your house. For example, he was only hired to come in and to look for any kind of proof. Maybe Dean hired this guy, not expecting him to get caught, because he's trying to do a court case and didn't think you would cooperate."

She sat back and stared at him. "I didn't even think of that, but, if that were the case, he couldn't have had anything to do with my parents' murder, right?"

"It's hard to say. Again we're just grasping at straws, hoping that somebody gives us enough information to take the next step."

She got up, walked over to the cupboard, pulled out a package of cookies, and came back to the table. "I'll put on a pot of tea, but somehow I don't think that's your drink."

"No, sure isn't. But, if you have plenty of coffee, I'll put on another pot."

She smiled. "I thought you might. Go ahead. We can always pick up more groceries tomorrow."

"That's what I was thinking too. I only bought enough for a couple meals, thinking that, depending on whatever else we need, we can make a run to the store."

She hesitated, then looked over at him, dropping her gaze.

"What's the matter?" he asked.

She shook her head. "Oh, it's foolish. I mean, it doesn't make any sense, but I was wondering how long you'll stick around."

"Until we get some answers anyway," he replied comfortably.

She stared at him. "You do know that answers may not come."

"They'll come eventually," he said. "We just can't be sure that they'll come anytime soon. It could be that you're good and ready for me to leave long before we get answers."

She nodded.

"So, if that turns out to be the case, do me a favor and let me know. I can always move out to a hotel."

She stared at him. "Seriously?"

"Sure, why not?" he asked. "I'm not here to make you uncomfortable."

"No, it's just the opposite. Having you here makes me comfortable, and I'm just a little worried I'll become too comfortable."

He stared at her for a long moment, and then slowly nodded. "I get that too. You're getting a certain level of comfort from knowing that you're not alone. It should also help though, at least I'm hoping it gives you enough comfort to maybe get some sleep."

"You figured that out too, *huh?*"

"That you probably haven't slept in years? Yeah, it wasn't that hard. Once you start getting into a stressful scenario, it's almost as if you begin to sleep with one eye open because you don't know where the next problem will come from or how to deal with it. I'm really not trying to make your life more complex. I'm trying to make it easier."

"And I really appreciate it, but, ever since the one guy was in the house without me knowing it, along with everything else, it's been pretty tough to get my mind wrapped around it all."

"Not to mention the fact that you were attacked," he added.

At that, she nodded. "Something else that I assume you know is that, just when I think I'm fine, I realize that maybe I'm not."

"In your position, being not so fine is really okay. This whole thing is a process, and the best thing we can do to make you feel better about it is to deal with it once and for all."

"Oh, I agree. I'm just not sure how we're supposed to get that done."

He smiled at her. "Let's deal with what we have in front of us. We'll park all discussions about me leaving for the moment, but, if you ever feel like you need me to leave, then tell me, and I'll go find another place to stay. No hard feelings."

"I doubt your bosses would want to cover that expense," she said, "and I don't want you to leave anyway. I would feel terrible if you were staying here to help me, and I couldn't even offer you a place to stay."

He shrugged. "I could even go camping if it came to that," he suggested.

"Good Lord, no," she said. "That would be foolish and would probably make me really mad to boot."

He laughed. "I don't know about foolish. Camping is a great pastime."

"Maybe, but I wouldn't know. I've never been camping in my life."

At that, he stared at her like she was some alien who had stumbled into his world.

"Hey, my parents weren't the outdoorsy kind of people," she explained. "They were more studious types, you know? Going to summer camps for me was about attending education programs held on campuses. We stayed in the dorms. Even still, I was a great disappointment to them."

"I doubt that," he argued instantly. "Parents may wish for something, but I don't think they write off a child because they want something completely different."

She laughed. "I used to tell them I was a disappointment all the time, and they would never let me get away with it," she said, with a smile. "It's really hard, and I know I should be over it by now, but sometimes? Well, … I miss them so much."

He nodded instantly. "Grief is something that never really leaves, and it's not a case of getting over it or a fear of forgetting about them. It's a case of honoring them and moving on in spite of it."

She reached for a cookie and immediately chomped on

it.

He laughed as he got up and poured himself a cup of coffee. "So, is there anything you want to do this evening?"

"I'd really like to go out in the back and do some work with my dogs," she replied, "but I have to admit that, since I got hurt, it's all been a little unnerving."

"Well, I'll work here in the house because I want to do some research of my own on these names that we got, plus I need to reread some of that paperwork."

She winced as she glanced at the paperwork from the attic. "And just like that, it's all back again. I managed to forget about it for all of five minutes."

"You go outside with the animals," he urged. "I'll stay in here and work on this." She hesitated, and he brushed her aside. "Go on."

Almost immediately Carly felt a sense of relief radiating off her. She quickly bounced to her feet. "If you don't mind."

"I don't mind a bit."

As she walked to the door, Shelby looked up at him, over at Carly, then walked back to him and lay down at his feet. She frowned. "I guess Shelby really knows that you understand her, doesn't she?"

"*Hmm*, I think she knows that something is going on around us, and she's uneasy because she doesn't know what it is."

"Well, since I have work to do with the others, are you okay if I leave her in here?"

"Sure. I'll come out with her in a little bit."

Carly nodded, and, with a hesitant glance at the dog, obviously not comfortable leaving her behind, or with Shelby choosing him for the moment, Carly went outside.

Declan looked down at Shelby. "What's the matter, girl?" he asked. "Something's obviously bothering you." Shelby immediately whined in the back of her throat, and, hearing that, he got up.

"Show me." Shelby bolted to her feet and raced toward the attic.

CHAPTER 6

ABOUT AN HOUR later, breathless and finding her center of peace again, Carly threw herself down onto the ground and let the dogs completely run over her. Laughing and giggling, she gave them all big cuddles. Rather than do a lot of serious work with them as much as she had just enjoyed them. She needed to get out and to have that release from the stress, knowing that things in her world were much better with Declan here. She didn't have a headache, and her stomach was full and happy, which said a lot about his cooking.

As a matter of fact, there was a hell of a lot to like about the man, not just his cooking. More than that was the lovely vibe that existed between them. Thankfully that seemed to have returned full force, despite her serious faux pas in questioning his fighting abilities with his prosthetic foot. *I'll never do that again*, she thought.

He was somebody she appreciated. She enjoyed his sense of humor, as well as his logical mind and that can-do attitude, which was not so different than that of her parents. They had been so tuned in to the academic and intellectual world, made even more rigid within the military parameters, whereas she had always been a free spirit.

Even now, successfully doing what she was doing with her animals and the patients, she didn't think her parents would approve. But since they were no longer around to frown on her choices, it really wasn't an issue. Yet, even to say it wasn't an issue almost felt like betraying them in some way, and she didn't want to feel that either. Despite those thoughts, something was very freeing about having Declan around.

His attitude, his complete acceptance of her and her dogs and her life, and the solid security level that he offered was a gift she didn't want to take advantage of, but, at the same time, she craved it. What she really craved was the normality, something she hadn't experienced in a very long time.

How sad was it to think that everything in her life had been such a mess that she didn't even know what *normal* meant anymore? She loved her parents dearly, but Carly had always felt a bit of a disconnect, knowing that she wasn't like them at all. Not that they didn't love her anyway, but she definitely had a sense of letting them down because she was different, because she didn't want to walk the same path they had walked.

She didn't want to be in the same drama that they were playing the lead in. She had to be herself, and her choices for college had been a large part of that. Going into a business field as she had chosen for her college degree flew in the face of their goals for her. They wanted her to do something staid and applicable, something that would make her employable. Trouble was, everything her parents wanted for Carly from the get-go was something that stifled her, making her feel like her whole world was coming to an end.

It had been a frightfully scary time when she realized that the family she had depended on her whole life and all the stability in her world were just gone. She didn't know what to do for the longest time. She had more or less stayed at home and done nothing, except functioned the best she could on a day-to-day basis, dealing with the problems that were in her face. But, for some problems, there was nothing to be done.

As she relaxed out back with the dogs, she looked up at the house and smiled. It had been a good choice to come out here. She had needed a break. Yet as she stared up at the house, she thought she caught sight of something on the top floor, curtains moving. Why the hell were there even curtains in the attic to begin with? She didn't know.

As she frowned, she focused and saw somebody waving at her, realizing it was Declan. She immediately lifted a hand and waved.

He poked his head out the window and called out, "I'll be down in a minute."

She nodded and just stayed here, relaxing. Something was so strange about not being alone. It had been a very long time since that had been part of her experience. She liked having someone around her.

After the loss of her parents, Carly had worried about being able to trust people without becoming completely dependent on somebody. She ended up in very strange dysfunctional relationships until she finally broke them off, telling people she just needed time to get her shit together.

She had needed time all right, though she wasn't sure she had the time. Yet, she'd taken years regardless. Having Declan here made her realize just how dysfunctional those other relationships had been and how far she'd come now. When she looked at him, she saw something completely different—a damn good thing, considering they weren't even in a relationship. She almost smiled at herself for that.

Something was very sweet and protective about him. She knew he would hate the word *sweet*, but, at the same time, it fit. Seemed to her a breed of males who were protectors were out there, whether they liked it or not, and also that a breed of women out there were looking for that protector.

Carly would never, ever consider herself to be in that category, yet she had to wonder if she hadn't fallen into that to some degree. It would be a very strange thing if that were to occur.

She had never really been comfortable with that role, but everything in her world had morphed. She'd had one world before her parents were murdered, then another world afterward. It was the latter that she was still trying to come to terms with.

She'd basically packed up and run, getting away from everything, and it had taken months, even years to actually calm down enough to create a somewhat normal life. It had taken a lot out of her to settle into something she was comfortable with. And, more than that, the difficult parts of her life were something she had stashed away and had put behind her, moving on—until all this headache happened, and Declan showed up in her world.

Now she had a completely different thought process in her mind, a completely different vision of who she was. Yet it wasn't a bad vision, and she was aware that something had changed within her. That development was even more bizarre, and she wasn't sure what to think or to feel.

She remained out in the grass, watching as Declan opened up the back door of the kitchen and stepped out to see her. Something was in his hands, and, as he got closer, she looked at the pop can, puzzled, and asked, "Oh, when did you pick that up?" And why was he holding it by a baggie?

"That's a good question." He smirked. "I would ask whether this is something you keep in the house."

She shrugged. "Can't remember the last time I had pop actually. I used to drink so much of it and finally got quite sick of it at college, so now I no longer have a taste for it."

"Got it, and I hadn't seen any around, which is why this is of particular interest."

"Yeah, why?" she asked, looking at him curiously.

"I found it in the attic," he stated, as he held it up. She stared at it, surprised. "Or rather Shelby did."

"I sure don't remember seeing it up there," Carly noted.

"Did you have some workers help move things up?"

She shook her head. "No, I didn't. I moved all that stuff up there myself. I did have a company help move me into the house, with all the heavier pieces, so it's quite possible that it came in then, depending on where you saw it. After somebody destroyed my attic and stirred everything up, who knows where it came from."

He nodded. "Do you mind if I send it off for prints?"

She stared at him in shock, then realizing what he was saying. "Fingerprints? Good God, you really think somebody would come in my house and go up to my attic, drink in hand, and leave it behind?"

"Well, it would also possibly explain why the guy was here. Maybe he came to collect this can. Maybe he was the one here and had left it," Declan theorized. "It's expensive to get it tested in a private lab, and, of course, we don't have anything to test it against, but—"

"You do whatever you want with it," she replied quickly. "I'm not even sure I want to know what the result is," she added ominously, then shook her head. "Of course I do, sorry. God, this is making me crazy."

"I'm not trying to make you crazy. I just found it odd that it would be up there." He gave it a shake, and she noted liquid was still in it. At that, her stomach sank even more.

Declan nodded, as if knowing what she was thinking. "If it had been there a long time, that would have evaporated. I suspect, for the little bit that's in the can now, it would have evaporated over the winter. However, it's May. So I would have suspected it would have even evaporated within a couple months."

"Great, but we're also assuming that it wasn't half full to begin with, right?"

He smiled. "I really enjoy your quick wit," he noted affectionately.

She snorted. "Honestly, right now, I'm not feeling like there's any quick wit involved," she mumbled. "This is just another step I don't want to consider."

"I get that, which is why I'm wondering about sending it down to my boss."

She wrapped her arms around her chest and sat up. "You do whatever you feel you need to do. I didn't tell the cops about the break-in, and I don't really know that they'll be too interested in that either."

"Considering where I found it, no," Declan agreed, "except for the fact that there was a lot of damage upstairs." He pulled out his phone and sent off a text.

"I presume that was to your boss?"

He nodded. "Yeah. I don't think he'll run DNA, and I don't know what he'll recommend in terms of local law enforcement."

She shrugged. "You know? I think local law enforcement here is as effective as any. I just don't think they have the resources for cases when there was no significant damage beyond some personal property."

"Yet it was files belonging to your parents, not just the court-martial of Dean but of the original police investigation of the murder."

"I know," she replied, yet not moved to bring in the local cops.

At that, he shrugged. "Well, I've sent off a request to Badger, so we'll see what he says."

"Good enough." Carly noticed that the entire energy out here had changed. She watched as Shelby wandered around the perimeter of the property. "Do you think she's looking for somebody?"

"I think she's just looking, checking, keeping an eye on things," Declan explained. "We need to just let her do that."

Carly looked over at him. "I never thought about what it would be like to have a real watchdog around the house."

"She's good," he stated. "I haven't got a list of her training and what's she's specialized in yet because that's part of what they're supposed to let go of when they come over to the civilian side, but it would be helpful to know what she's capable of doing." He looked down at Carly and asked, "Are you ready for bed?"

"No," she said instantly, and then she winced. "And yet I should be, shouldn't I? It all just feels very strange now."

"I've checked out the upstairs, closed a few doors, and everything out front is locked. It's getting dark out already, but it sure is beautiful out here."

"It is, indeed," she murmured. "That's why I was lying here, looking up at the sky, thinking that moving here had been such a great thing, but now I'm not feeling that way at all."

"Of course, and I'm sorry. I didn't mean to shake you out of that hard-earned complacency.'

"Well, maybe it was a good thing because, even at that, I never found peace. I certainly don't want to get too complacent and end up in more trouble."

He didn't say anything to that, for which she was grateful. He reached out a hand to help her up off the ground, but, rather than her using it to get up, she gave it a hard tug, making him stumble down beside her. Too late, she remembered his prosthetic, but thankfully he was laughing as he landed by her.

"You could have just asked me to sit down, you know?" he told her in a mocking tone.

"I should have." Yet she was laughing, feeling so relieved that he wasn't offended. She hadn't really considered if he was able-bodied before she jerked on his hand. However, even as she had the thought, she knew he would be insulted. Because he was an amputee, it seemed that everything was different, and yet it shouldn't be; it shouldn't be different at all. Still, somehow it was. She fell back down on the grass, looking up at the sky. "How does one ever let go of the reminder that somebody was in your house, going through your things, looking for something?"

"In this case, the best answer is to find out who it was and why they were there, then see if you can come to terms with it that way. Otherwise there'll always be that sense of invasion, of somebody taking advantage. Somebody is out there, who's come into your space, who didn't belong there," Declan stated. "I'm not sure there's any easy answer except time and resolution of the matter. And there is always therapy, if you think you need it."

She snorted at that. "I can just imagine the therapy session, explaining all this. No thanks. Not something I'm particularly fond of anyway."

"Did you go for therapy after you lost your parents?"

"I did. I was away at school at the time of their deaths, so it was hard to find any closure," she shared. "That was something I struggled with. So I did talk to somebody for a bit, but you know? At some point in time, that has to come to an end."

"I guess it does," he agreed.

"What about you? Did you?"

"Yeah, because, just like you, it was the ending of life as I knew it," he explained. "It was the end of my career, the end of everything in many ways. I had friends who had already gone through something similar, and I think that helped, but it wasn't the kind of thing I wanted to run around asking for help with."

"No, of course not. We're not very good at asking for help, are we?"

He chuckled. "I'm certainly not, although I've been getting better at it."

They stayed outside for a long time, until she finally muttered, "I think I need to go to bed now."

"You do. Come on. Let's get you upstairs." Then he helped her up, and they walked back to the house. "Any more headaches?"

She shook her head. "No, it's actually been pretty decent today."

"Good, that will really help."

"Maybe. Yet at the same time, it feels like nothing will really help."

"Finding the answers is the key. As somebody who's been there and done that, I can tell you that finding answers is what helps."

THE NEXT MORNING Declan got up, put on the coffee, and wandered through the house. Everything outside appeared calm, yet a sense of disquiet hung in the air. He didn't know what it was, but it had woken him up, taking him from a sound sleep to awake and aware within minutes. Now dressed, and not seeing anything that his senses told him was going on, he looked down at Shelby to find her in the same situation, her sense of awareness heightened.

"Something's out there, isn't it?" he murmured. She looked at him and her tail wagged, and immediately her gaze went to the kitchen door.

"You want to go out?" he asked. At her tiny *woof*, he opened the door, and, with a cup of coffee in hand, he stepped out with her. She stopped at the top step of the deck and looked around. Her ears were up. Her tail didn't wag, and her inner sense—which he knew perfectly well that dogs did have—knew something unnerving was out there. Declan watched as she slowly made her way down to the yard and went to the bathroom.

When she was done, she continued on to the back of the fence. Her ears up, her gaze scanned from side to side as she moved. He watched her, knowing that she would tell him faster than anything when something was wrong. She got down to the far back side and seemed to relax, and he felt some of his own tension relaxing along with hers. Then suddenly she bounded forward and started barking. He raced down and joined her at the back fence, looking to see what had her upset. The fact that she'd calmed down and then had barked confused him. He didn't know if it was just a change in wind direction or if she had missed something earlier.

Whatever it was, she was pretty upset about it right now. He got down and placed a hand on her shoulder, as he studied the area around him. Hanging off the end of the fence was a dead squirrel. He looked at it for a long moment, then realized the squirrel hadn't come to its end naturally. It had actually been hooked on the fence.

He quickly took several photos and sent them off to Badger, who called him right away.

"That's an odd threat," he murmured.

"I know, and it doesn't make any sense. Yet there's definitely a feeling of this not being there before."

"Had you been along that back fence before?"

"No, and believe me I wish I had been," Declan admitted. "There's a weird sensation of being watched, plus that pop can I found yesterday. And, as you mentioned, no way to really know how long it had been there."

"Believe me. I know those instincts. Keep listening to them," Badger replied. "This is just one of those odd situations where we still don't quite understand what we're looking for."

"As to anything and anyone," Declan stated, his tone abrupt.

"Look. I'll phone the local cops in town and see if I can catch a guy I've been to a couple conferences with. Hopefully he'll come out and talk to you guys." With that, Badger hung up, leaving Declan staring down at the phone, wondering just what was going on.

When he got back into the house, Carly stood at the rear doorway, a robe wrapped around her.

"What's the matter?" she asked him.

"Shelby found a dead squirrel on your fence," he told her.

Her gaze widened. "Like somebody did that, or was it a natural death?"

"I'll say somebody did it," he said. "What is interesting is that the fence is that far away from the house, and it doesn't look like it's a terribly fresh kill, but I can't be sure."

She nodded. "Wow, so this is what I'll have to see now? People tormenting animals and hanging them on my fence?"

"The question is why though. That's really the concern." He walked back into the kitchen, poured her a cup of coffee, and handed it to her. "Here. Have a cup of coffee. We might get some company, but I don't know for sure."

She stared at him. "Well, that was kind of nebulous, and I'm not at all sure what you mean."

"Sorry. My boss is trying to reach out to somebody he knows on the local police force. I don't know whether Badger will make that connection or not, but chances are he will, and, in that case, the local guy may come by."

"*Great*, I'm not sure I have much rapport with anybody local."

"Yet you have spoken to the cops about the attack on you," he added. "It's also kind of odd that we haven't heard anything back from them."

"Not necessarily odd if they don't have anything to say. I'm pretty sure they're happy I'm not the kind of person to be phoning steadily."

"Well, as it turns out, I *am* the kind of person who will phone steadily," he quipped, "particularly if there is a lack of due diligence in their investigation."

"What are they supposed to investigate?" she asked, with

half a smile. "You might want to keep that in mind."

"Oh, I know, but it will still be interesting to see who shows up."

"Are you really expecting somebody to come just because your boss says so?"

Declan smiled at her. "Yeah, you don't know how they operate."

"No, I sure don't"—she sighed—"but it would be nice if I did. It would be nice to think that there might be some answers somewhere because I don't really feel that I got anywhere as far as my parents are concerned."

"Well, you didn't, and that's something we'll have to talk to the authorities about too."

"It was a different state though."

"Yeah, I know, and that just compounds it all. However, we'll get there. We will. It's just a matter of time."

She nodded and didn't say anything, then looked down at herself. "In that case I better go get changed." She picked up her coffee and headed upstairs. While she was upstairs, and, with that sense of something impending, Declan quickly cooked up some bacon and eggs. By the time she came back down, it was ready.

She shook her head. "As house guests go, you are to die for."

He laughed. "Always happy to help out."

"Well, there's helping and there's completely looking after me," she noted. "I can't say I've ever really had anybody do that."

"At least since your mom anyway, *huh*?"

"Nope, my mother was not the domestic type," she admitted, with a bright smile.

Sure enough, by the time they sat down and finished

eating, they heard a vehicle approaching.

She looked up at him. "Is that your person?"

"I have no idea. No clue what's coming."

She winced at that. "Jesus, let's just hope it's the cops and not a drive-by shooting or something," she muttered in a dark tone. He looked at her in surprise. She shrugged. "Hey, it's been a rough go."

He nodded. "Let's just hold those kind of comments for the moment, and we'll see what ends up transpiring." He got up and walked out to the front of the house and stood there, as an unmarked police car pulled up. He looked down at her when she joined him.

"Wow, somebody showed up. That's pretty impressive, since it's more than I could get done in all this time. Kudos to your boss."

He laughed. "It's not kudos he wants. It's answers."

"He sounds like somebody I'll like to meet," she murmured. "If only life were quite so simple."

"It might not be that simple, but you also don't have to stay here, unless you want to."

She looked at him in surprise and then shrugged. "It hasn't been a bad place to be, until this came up."

"Until somebody found you again." He looked at her sharply. "Did you by any chance contact anyone who could have let somebody know where you were currently?"

She frowned at him in surprise and shook her head. "No, I don't think so. I mean, it's not something that I necessarily was trying to hide, but I also didn't think I would be on anybody's radar for this long either."

"Right. Well, we may have to take another look at that."

When the lower gate at the front of the yard opened, a man in plainclothes stepped up. He smiled at them. "Declan, by chance?"

He nodded. "Yes, that's me." At that, his phone buzzed. He pulled it out to see a message from Badger, giving the guy's name to Declan. "You don't mind if I have a look at your badge, do you?"

"Not a problem, if that's what you want." He pulled it out enough for Declan to confirm it matched the name on his phone.

"Thanks for coming, Larry. I don't know how much you know about this mess."

"Not enough, from the sounds of it," he stated, looking over at Carly. "I understand there was an attack here a couple days ago?"

At that, she nodded slowly. "Yes, I was attacked by an intruder. Actually Declan here found me and called 9-1-1 and got the ball rolling, after he got me some medical attention."

"You were knocked out?" he asked sharply.

"Yes, hit from behind actually." At that, she reached up a hand, winced, and said, "I can't say it's completely healed yet either."

"Head wounds can take a bit of time to get there," Larry confirmed. "They're often irritating as hell, and then, all of a sudden, you forget about them because they're that much further down the healing road."

"Well, that would be nice, but I'm apparently not there yet."

He smiled, as she stepped back and offered, "Would you like some coffee?"

"I'd love one, thank you," he said easily. He followed them and stepped into the house and looked around. The dogs immediately milled around checking the new arrival but at Declan's orders, they let Larry inside.

Declan noted Larry was assessing the security on the place. "She doesn't have any security system or cameras," Declan confirmed immediately.

Larry nodded. "I never understand that."

"No, but I think money may have been a part of it and then a misplaced sense of trying to get control in her life."

At that, Larry looked at him in surprise. "Sorry?"

"Yeah, she'll have to explain that to you because I still don't understand myself." Declan chuckled.

Obviously she had heard him, since she came out glaring in his direction. "There are some things you might need to know," she told Larry. "I don't see how any of it is related or if it's got nothing to do with anything," she began, "but Declan thinks there has got to be some connection to my past troubles."

"Well, in that case, yeah, we need to get filled in," Larry agreed. "So, did you tell the first cops what you're about to tell me?"

She shook her head. "Honestly, I haven't had anybody back to even ask me any questions about it."

He stared at her. "Nobody came to follow up, after you were attacked in your own home?"

She nodded. "Yeah, and I wasn't sure what I was supposed to do about that. Declan here seems to think that I should have been hounding you."

Larry winced at that. "Well, we don't want to get hounded, that's for sure, but there should have been some sort of follow-up questions. If you didn't go to the hospital, maybe they didn't think it was that major."

"Maybe," she hedged, "although somebody still entered my home and hit me over the head."

Larry nodded. "I'll bring it up with my supervisors, when I get back, but whatever you can tell me right now would be helpful."

She looked over at Declan and then shrugged. "Honestly I don't even know where to start. It's kind of convoluted."

Declan shook his head. "It's really not convoluted at all. A couple issues are here, and we don't know if they are connected or not. First off, when I initially came to see her, I saw a young man leaving this property. I was still driving and looking to find the right address, so I didn't think much of it." He went on to explain what had happened next and then continued. "As she answered my questions, while I tried to figure out a motive for the attack, one of the things that came out was the fact that her parents were murdered."

At that, the detective straightened up in his chair and frowned at her.

Declan added, "The case was never solved."

The detective whistled. "Yeah, I can see now why you would wonder about a connection."

"So, now we need to fill you in on that," Declan stated, and he proceeded to take charge and succinctly give Larry as much of the information as possible, about both the murders and also Dean's military trial. "Because of what we were considering, we reached out to the person who was convicted and served his sentence, based on the testimony of her parents. We saw him yesterday."

The detective just stared at him. "Sounds like you don't even need a cop."

"I do," Declan clarified, "because it's starting to get a little murky now." By the time he finished explaining what he could, including the vehicle following them, finding the pop can up in the attic yesterday, and then the dead squirrel on the fence this morning, the detective sat back and stared down at his several pages of notes.

"Wow. It'll take a little bit to get my mind wrapped around all this."

"Yeah, it's been taking us a little bit to do that too," she quipped, on a wry note.

"If only it was that easy to sort some of this stuff out. So, what did you do with the can?"

"The can is still here." Declan got up, walked to the kitchen, picked up the bagged can, and brought it back out again.

"Well, that's good." By the time Larry asked a few more questions of them, he looked over at Declan. "So, Badger called me."

"Yeah, I know he did."

"He's a good man and not prone to hysteria," he noted, "for lack of a better word." Then Larry grinned. "Do tell him I said that."

"Oh, I'll be sure to." Declan chuckled. "I'm certain that will raise all kinds of eyebrows. I can't wait."

"Kat is a really good person too," Larry added, "but honestly this isn't something that should have required a phone call from them in order to get some traction on this case. Honest to God, you should have gotten a follow-up call and a visit right away."

"Well, it's only been two days, but I would have thought so, yeah," Declan agreed.

Larry looked at the bag with the pop can. "I don't know that anybody's got the budget for something like this though."

"I understand," Declan replied. "Now let me ask you something. If she had been more seriously injured and wound up in the hospital, would you have the resources then?"

The detective winced. "*Right.* It's mostly about what our chances are to get a conviction."

"I get it," Carly interjected, "but as somebody who's already been put through the wringer and back over a case that still hasn't left me alone, it would be awfully nice if somebody would give a crap."

"Oh, I care"—Larry nodded—"but trying to get some of this stuff tested will run through the department's budget money pretty fast."

Declan frowned. "And, I guess from your perspective, you don't have any way of knowing for sure that it was from the guy who was up there."

"No, but then again, who else would it have been?" Carly countered. "Neither of us drank it. I've lived here for a few years and haven't had any workmen or anything up there. Yet we do know we had an intruder trashing my attic. All of which lends weight to it potentially being relevant."

Larry sighed. "I'll have to take it to my boss and see what he says."

"Make sure he gives you the right answer," Declan noted, his tone cool. "I can't say it'll go over that well to have the police holding back their resources from a B&E case that resulted in the physical assault on an innocent resident of your town—and a single woman living alone—who nobody followed up to investigate."

"And all that will give it weight," Larry assured them.

"I'm just telling you that," Declan explained, "I've heard a lot of this kind of guff before."

The detective nodded. "Whether we like it or not, our resources are limited, and using them in the most prudent way we can is something that we always have to keep in mind."

"Oh, I get it, have heard it before," Declan replied. "Yet the fact of the matter is, we still have a problem, and we're really hoping that we can get her some help."

Larry nodded. "What kind of help are you thinking of?"

At that, she stood. "It's a waste of time, isn't it? Do you have any idea what I went through? That man was in my home, and I don't even know how many times. Or for the other matter, what I endured and still do to this day over my parents' murder? We got nowhere, and the murderer is still out there. To me, it feels very much like that's happening all over again." And, with that, she got up and walked out.

Declan looked over at the detective. "It would be nice if her faith in law enforcement could be reinforced this time. So far, this has just reinforced her belief that she's on her own, just like she has been since somebody decided to kill her parents six years ago."

Larry sighed. "I feel for her, but it's not that easy, and you know it."

"I sure do, but I also know that she's been completely devastated over what's happened in her life, and some asshole is still playing games with her. Now it's become an attack in her home and dead animals left for her by this nutjob."

"What are the chances of that squirrel being put there was for a different reason?" the detective asked.

"I wondered that myself," Declan noted, immediately understanding the question.

"I don't get it. What are you saying?" Carly asked from the doorway.

He looked over at her and winced. "I guess I was wondering if it was left on the fence because of Shelby, otherwise it would have ended up inside the house or at least closer."

"Right," she muttered, "so just in case I didn't see it, my tormenter would have brought it in closer."

"Something like that," Declan agreed. "It could also just be yet another warning, he didn't know what he would do with it, so putting it there was a casual idea that he just ran with."

"But does this seem like somebody who's just running with something like that on the spur of the moment?" she asked curiously.

"Well, it's not exactly methodical and thought out, is it?" Declan asked. "So we have to assume either that he's just winging it or that he's trying to see what we know or what we have and just wants to get you out of the house."

"Well, that kind of thing is more likely to *stop* me from getting out of the house," she replied. "I don't have security or anything, so I won't know if anybody is in here while I'm gone."

"That is something we'll work on today," Declan stated. "I had Badger ship me some simple security equipment that will at least give us some idea of what's going on. It's not superexpensive, and, once we get it set up, we'll get video surveillance of activity around the place—depending on how many cameras he's sending of course."

"That's—" She stopped as if unsure what to say.

"I know how many I asked for," Declan shared, and then he just shrugged. "I just don't know how many we'll get."

"Right. Largely because this is completely unrelated to what you were sent here for."

"Exactly."

She slowly sagged into the chair beside the detective.

"Any help would be much appreciated," she told him, turning to face him, her tone more formal than expected.

The detective nodded. "We obviously need to find out who broke into your house and attacked you," he said, his tone gentle. "And, if this is related to anything else going on with your family, then clearly we need to get to the bottom of it."

"As fast as possible. I feel like I'm on borrowed time in a way," she shared. "Though it all just seems so damn farfetched. Even if this whole mess is somehow related to the murder of my parents, or even if—and that's a big *if*—it could be related to Dean's conviction, I still don't get why."

"But," Declan began, "what you don't necessarily see right now is that for somebody who's gotten away with what he did in terms of treason, then potentially adding two murders to his rap sheet to cover up the treason, then the stakes have never been higher than they are right now—since Dean is out of prison and initiating a new investigation. People can get pretty desperate when they think of getting caught and having to spend the rest of their lives behind bars."

The detective nodded. "Not to mention, if he's connected to the military charges, that is serious business, and they'll have quite a bit to say about the whole thing. Depending on his age, this guy may never see the light of day again."

She nodded slowly. "Not a nice thought, is it?"

"Not a nice thought for him, but it would bring a measure of peace to you," Declan pointed out. "We will get to the bottom of this."

She gave him a wan smile. "Thanks for the vote of confidence because—I've got to admit right about now—the chances are looking kind of slim."

"No, not at all," Declan argued. "Your intruder saw that I was here. Your intruder saw the dog was here, and he didn't do anything more than drop a squirrel on a fence."

"Maybe," she murmured. "I get that I'm not supposed to be upset about a squirrel, but there's really no part of my life where it's okay to do that to an animal, regardless of how small or insignificant it might seem to somebody else."

"Right, and I know that," Declan told her. "That's also probably what this guy is expecting. And we don't even know that the squirrel was even killed by him. For all we know, it was hit by a vehicle."

"Actually I would ask to see it anyway," the detective stated.

At that, Declan nodded. "I'll take you out back." And, with that, the two of them headed out through the kitchen door. As Declan walked out, he looked back to speak to her. "If you don't mind, just stay here."

She nodded. "I'll keep the dogs." And, with all the dogs inside with her, Declan walked out with the detective.

CHAPTER 7

AFTER THE DETECTIVE left, it was hard for Carly to stay positive, not with so much shit going on in her world. As Declan came back in, she asked, "Did Larry take the pop can?"

Declan nodded. "He did."

"He didn't look very happy about it."

Declan laughed. "Doesn't matter whether he's happy or not. He did tell us that he would try, and he took it. Now it's up to him to do what he has to do."

She sighed. "I guess it's not fair to hold what happened to me against them, is it?"

"No, but it's an understandable and common reaction, and it is part of their job, so don't be too hard on yourself."

She shrugged irritably. "It's not even that. I just want it all to be over with."

"Got it," he said cheerfully. "Anyway, while I was outside, I got notification that the security equipment I ordered has arrived."

She looked at him in surprise. "He actually sent it?"

"Sure." Declan nodded. "I need to go into town and pick it up."

"Right." She frowned, looking around. "You better go do that then."

"I don't want to leave you alone."

She snorted. "You'll have to leave me alone at some point in time, so we might as well get it over with." When he hesitated, she just waved at him. "Go on. I'm feeling out of sorts as it is. Just go do what you need to do."

When he hesitated again, she faced him with a frown. "Look. I can't go with you and leave everything here for the intruder to go through again or to camp out in my attic. That's not smart. You go, and I'll keep all the dogs with me. I promise I'll keep Shelby close."

He nodded at that. "Okay, that works, and, as much as I hate it, that would be the most efficient answer. Though I could see about getting a delivery to your house later."

"Don't be silly." She waved her hand again. "Let's just get this done, and then we can begin to move on," With that, she watched as he headed out to his truck. Shelby stayed at Carly's side, and Declan took off. She looked down at the beautiful dog. "Well, it's just like before, girl," Carly noted, "just the two of us, but that's okay. Sometimes that's just the way life is." Then she headed back inside and started doing the dishes.

When her phone rang, instinctively thinking it was Declan, she answered, "Hello, Declan. What's the matter?"

"Well, it's not Declan," the man stated, "but I highly suggest you leave town." And, with that, whoever it was hung up.

She stared down at the phone, her heart sinking. "Jesus," she muttered. Unsure if she should phone Declan or not, she realized the caller had a Private Number designation. She wasn't sure what to do with that. She thought there might have been some way to get the number from her phone, but she didn't know how.

Not sure what to do, she walked over to her computer

and started a search, but it came up with nothing. Thinking she might have gotten it wrong, she ended up calling Declan after all. "I just had a threatening phone call," she told him.

"What happened?"

"Not very much. Someone, a man, just told me to get out of town, which makes no sense at all."

"Unless they're trying to get you scared enough to run."

"Why should I though? Actually, if that was their plan, it's backfiring. It's only making me furious instead."

He laughed. "That's a good thing," he murmured. "You need to get angry, but you also need to stay safe."

"I searched on the internet for how to look up a Private Number phone number of who just called, but it didn't work."

"Well, depending on how organized this mess is, chances are it wouldn't. It most likely would be a disposable phone. A burner phone, as they call it."

"Interesting. Well, I don't know what to say. All I can tell you is that it just happened, and, if he calls again, I won't answer."

"That's a good idea. I've picked up my stuff, and I'm actually on my way back to your place."

She hated the sense of relief that washed over her but immediately replied, "Well, I'm glad to hear that. I'll just go outside and work with the animals." And, with that, she hung up.

She headed outside and put them through what she had set up as fun neuroactive exercises for them. It wasn't for training as much as for getting them to do what they needed to do. In this case, it had nothing to do with anything except her own mental health.

Outside, with the animals running and dashing about,

she laughed several times, feeling her mood lighten a bit. When she heard a vehicle out front, she looked over at Shelby to see her standing and staring at the front yard. "Is it him?" she asked Shelby.

Shelby looked at her, gave a *woof*, her tail wagging like crazy, as she raced to the front gate. "I'll take that as a yes. That's a good sign if nothing else," she murmured. It was also a sign that Shelby was quickly becoming quite attached to Declan, which gave Carly an odd feeling, considering that she had been with Shelby longer. But then animals were like that.

It also appeared that Shelby was quite happy with men. That was a good thing, especially if Shelby were to do therapy work because a lot of men liked big dogs, whereas a lot of women liked the little ones. Support dogs needed to work with any of them, and they couldn't be fussy. When they went into a hospital room or a rehab facility, the therapy dogs had to be completely okay to be with whatever person was on the other side of that door.

When she looked back at the house, Declan walked her way, Shelby racing toward him. Carly smiled.

Declan called out, "Now that's a good welcome." He bent down and spent several moments just cuddling Shelby.

It kind of gave Carly's heart a pang, but still, if Shelby found somebody to love who would love her, then Carly was all for it. Carly joined them. "How much stuff is there to bring in?"

"I brought it in already, not a whole lot."

She nodded as she stepped into the kitchen behind him. "How much money do I owe you or whomever?"

"I'm not sure yet. I've been talking to Badger about it, trying to figure out what kind of money we're looking at."

"I presume you can take it back with you afterward?"

He nodded. "I could, but that's hardly the issue right now."

She pinched her lips together and nodded. "I'm just not really comfortable taking charity."

"It's not charity at the moment. It's safety," he pointed out. "I'm pretty sure you want to keep living, and I don't know what this guy is up to. I don't want to see how far he's prepared to go to keep his freedom, so let's just shelve any discussion about costs until later."

"I just don't have a ton of money," she said.

"I don't expect you to," he replied, looking at her in surprise. "Let's just take this one day at a time."

She nodded slowly. "Okay, but I can't say I'm very comfortable with it though."

He chuckled. "I get that. Come on. You can give me a hand putting it up." And together, they spent the next several hours setting up security cameras all around the property, cordless ones. With her on her laptop, he quickly adjusted the angles so that every approach was covered.

She stared at it all in amazement. "Wow, I didn't know you could get something like this."

"And it's not always what they try to sell you, if you were shopping in person for it either," he pointed out, "but this seems like a good idea for you right now."

She couldn't argue with that. "I'm really happy to see all this." When the install was all done, she looked around. "Now what?"

"Now I've got to check in with my boss."

She winced. "Seems funny to have a boss." He looked at her in surprise. She shrugged. "I've been working on my own for quite a while now. Bosses were never my thing."

He burst out laughing. "Well, there are bosses, and then there are bosses. In this case, I'm pretty much a free agent."

"And what would you be doing if you weren't doing this?"

"Well, I won't be doing this long-term. This is kind of a one-off deal. They needed somebody to come check up on the War Dog and asked me if could help out. The rest? Well, that's a whole different story, as you well know."

She nodded, wrapping her arms around herself.

He immediately opened his arms. "Sorry, I didn't mean to upset you."

She shook her head but edged a bit closer.

He smiled, reached out, and tugged her into his arms for a hug, teasing her by saying, "You might not be too much of a hugger, but I am."

She chuckled. "I haven't really had much chance to be a hugger," she admitted. "My parents were definitely not huggers." He looked at her in surprise. She struggled to not laugh at the face he made. "Yes, I'm serious. Not everybody in the world is of the same ilk."

"Nope, not at all," he muttered. "I just didn't realize parents wouldn't be."

"Well, in my case they certainly were not," she declared, even with a smile. "Just a fact of life. I didn't really know what I was missing until much later, ... then I realized just how different I really was from them."

Declan hesitated, then asked, "Just to clear the air, they are your blood parents, right?"

Shocked, she stared at him. "I think so, yes. Surely, just because they weren't huggers, that doesn't mean that we're not blood kin."

"No. It was just a thought, and one of the many things

we're trying to find some rhyme or reason for regarding their murders, what may have transpired, and why."

"That would be something, wouldn't it? I would hate to think that my mother was murdered for having an affair and not telling somebody about an offspring."

Declan faced her. "Do you have any pictures of them?"

She frowned. "You're seriously wondering if I'm really their child, aren't you?"

He nodded. "Just to rule it out, you know?"

With him at her side, she walked into the room she used as her home office. Sitting down at the desk, she opened a drawer and pulled out several photographs. "These are my parents. I don't have them up because it always reminds me of their murders and the unsolved case, so I keep them in here. If I ever need that motivation to keep struggling through the world, I can just pull open this drawer and smile," she shared. "However, it hurts to see them sometimes."

"Of course it does. That is something that will change, once we get some answers."

"And I'm back to *if* we get answers," she replied.

"I know that you have doubts, and I understand why, but I hope you're wrong."

"I hope I'm wrong too. I hope you find exactly what's going on."

He looked back and forth from her to the photos several times. "Honestly I can't tell."

"What do you mean?" she asked, as she jumped to her feet and came around to his side. "Why would you even say that?" She stared down at the various photos of her parents, some with Dean and her too. "Surely I must look like them." She stared and pointed. "There. Look at my mother."

At that, he nodded. "Yeah, I can see that resemblance, but I sure don't see any resemblance to your father."

Her heart sinking, Carly snatched the photo out of his hands and took a closer look. "Sure there is." But even she was sensing some doubts. "Well, if he's not my blood father, I have absolutely no idea who is." At Declan's odd silence, she looked over at him. "What?" When he still didn't say anything and just stared at her steadily, she groaned. "You see? That is one of the looks I hate—when somebody knows something, but they don't want to tell you. They want you to figure it out for yourself, as if that will somehow be better. It's just BS, if you ask me."

His lips twitched. "I highly suspect that, if Henry isn't your blood father, we will have to do a DNA test in order to find out. If he's not, I suspect that we spoke to your father yesterday."

She stared at him in shock. "Dean? Why on earth would you think that?"

"One, because he was their best friend, so he would have been close and on the spot. Two, … your chin."

She grabbed a small hand mirror from her desk drawer. Looking into it, she had a dimple in the center of her chin and remembered that Dean had one as well. "Oh my God." She took a closer look at her cheekbones and the rest of her face. Her whisper was a hoarse roar, as she looked over at Declan. "Oh my God, you're right. Dean is my father." Declan reached out and pulled her into his arms, and she felt the tremble starting from her toes. "How could they lie to me like that?"

"I suspect Henry probably didn't know," Declan suggested. "I'm not sure Dean does either. Although, after meeting you yesterday, something odd was in his initial demeanor, but it seemed to calm down right afterward."

"Sure, but I thought that was"—she stopped a moment, then shook her head—"I thought it was just him. His way. He seemed surprised at meeting me, after all that time." She stared down at the family photo in shock. "It has to be wrong." She continued to shake her head. "It has to be."

"We may like to think so," Declan began, "but I am definitely suspicious as I look down at this photo." He hesitated, then added, "It would also be very convenient if Henry did find out and then got rid of Dean for all these years."

At that, she stared at him in shock. "But my mother? She went along with Dad. Oh no, please, please don't say that," she whispered. "I don't want to think that."

"I know. First things first. I think we'll need to get your DNA tested. Dean's should already be on file because of the criminal case, so there should be something on record."

She swallowed hard. "And if you're right?" She stared up at him. "What if Dean's innocent in all this? What if he lost out on having a family because of this?"

"Well, if he's innocent—and we have no proof either way," he reminded her. "None of us do. All we have is Dean's word, but, if he's innocent and if he didn't know about you, then he may or may not have understood better after meeting you yesterday. Still, he might have his suspicions."

"Of course he'll have suspicions," she snapped. "I didn't even see it myself until you pointed it out, but, once you did, it's pretty hard to deny." She sagged into her desk chair. "Right now I'm not very happy you did."

Declan nodded. "Again we're back down to needing answers, and we need the truth. So, buckle up for the ride.

We have to get to the bottom of this." And, with that, he picked up the phone and called the detective. As soon as he answered, Declan explained what they were currently wondering and asked him where they could get a DNA test.

DECLAN TOOK CARLY home after having her blood drawn and sent off to the lab. Now sitting on the back deck, waiting for the coffee to finish dripping, he looked at her calmly. "How are you feeling?"

"Pretty rough inside," she muttered. "I hope you're wrong because you know? It doesn't change anything in the sense that Henry was my father. He was there the whole time I was growing up, but I also can't see my mother having done something like that to him. To Henry or to Dean, not to mention to me."

"We also don't know what your parents' relationship was like, such as how much of it was happy and how much of it might have been more for show."

She winced at that. "There was a lot of coldness," she admitted. "It was one of the reasons I wasn't too keen on hanging around all that long after high school. I just felt like an odd fish."

"What are the chances that Henry knew about the affair?"

"I don't know," she stated. "We're just speculating, and I'm not prepared to say more until we know for sure."

"I let Badger know, and he's put a rush on the DNA results."

"But still, all these things cost money," she muttered.

"Well, we're really hoping that the local PD and the

sheriff's office will cover some of it. If not"—Declan shrugged—"I will."

She froze. "What? We need to find out the truth, so ... I'll pay for it," she stated. "My parents left me some money, so it seems appropriate, if not ironic, to use it to find out if they actually were my parents. God, what a mind-bender." But she scooted closer to him on the back deck, looped her arm with his. "I appreciate the offer of help with it, but I'm not destitute. I can afford both the security and the DNA test."

He nodded. "That's fine, if you're comfortable doing it. After all, I ordered the cameras without asking you first, and then I pretty well pushed you into taking the DNA test. Otherwise we'll look at the options."

"No, I am totally fine with it, particularly now. ... I can't even imagine. I can't even let myself go in that direction, yet it won't stop going there."

"That's pretty normal too. The waiting will be tough, but you've got this. However, sometimes the private labs are pretty fast, I think. Still, no telling what their backlog is like right now. Regardless we'll get there," he added, with a smile. "Try not to worry about it."

She groaned at that. "Now I'm hungry. We had a very skimpy lunch, you know?"

"Well, we have steak in the fridge," he reminded her. "Are you up for some barbecue?"

She grinned at him in delight. "Oh, I do like having you around. I can't even remember the last time I had a good steak."

He looked at her skeptically. "Seriously? Steaks are one of my favorite food groups."

She snorted at that, earning that smile she was becoming

so fond of.

"Before we start cooking, I was thinking maybe we could take Shelby and the others for a walk out back. Your property has a lot of acreage."

She nodded. "It's open land too. I have five acres here, which is more than enough, but only the section around the house here is fenced."

"Great, I'd love to see more of it. Let me get the steaks in the marinade, and then we'll grab the dogs and all go for a walk."

So, that's what they did. She played with the dogs inside, while he fussed with the steaks. As soon as he was done, he said, "Okay, let's get going." Surrounded by all the animals, he led the way out to the back, which happened to be where the squirrel had been. It had been removed, of course, but he didn't say anything to her about it, checking to make sure nothing else was troublesome.

Satisfied, he held out his hand to her. "Come on. Let's go enjoy a little time together."

She smiled and slipped her hand into his, and they headed out to enjoy a walk.

CHAPTER 8

CARLY FOUND THE next few hours to be some of the most relaxing and delightful hours she had experienced in a long time. As they settled in to have their steak dinner, she looked over at him and smiled. "I shouldn't be anywhere near this calm. I mean, all kinds of hell are breaking loose in my world, and yet ..." She shook her head, shrugged, then continued. "I know it sounds stupid, but I'm not as upset as I feel I should be."

"That's because you're not alone, for the first time in a very long while," he noted. "I know what that's like too. Facing problems like this all alone leaves you recalling all the details, calculating the potential risks and rewards, and making all the decisions in order to solve or even cope with a problem like this. I don't think anybody should be alone when it comes to these scenarios."

"Maybe not," she said, "but it sure seems like I've been alone for a very long time." He squeezed her hand, and she looked down at their joined fingers and smiled. "Even just this," she pointed out, squeezing his hand. "I'm not sure what the hell's going on between us, but this just feels right."

"I'm glad to hear you say that. I was afraid if I mentioned it first, it might scare you off."

After dinner, they stepped outside and wandered around the property, again with joined hands. "I don't usually move quickly in a relationship," she shared.

"I don't either, but sometimes it's just right. Sometimes you need to trust and jump in with both feet."

She chuckled. "Maybe so, and it feels right even now." She shrugged. "Odd, isn't it?"

"How about unusual, different, unique, or new instead?"

At that, she burst out laughing. "All of the above, yes. I guess I'm just not sure exactly what to say about it."

"Do we need to say anything?" he asked curiously.

She looked at him in surprise, and then shrugged. "You know what? Maybe not. Maybe we're okay to just keep moving through whatever this is."

"I am," he declared, "whatever it is. I think we've decided that we like who we are together."

"Yes," she agreed immediately. "It's just not something I expected."

"Well, walking into your house and finding you on the kitchen floor with your head bashed in wasn't what I expected either," he teased, with a half smile, "but I'm okay to just go with it."

Again she laughed out loud. "Providing it never happens again, I am too." She tried to contain her giggles at the ridiculous visual image his description had called to mind. That sense of feeling good was really strong. "This is almost, ... almost like being high right now. There's such a joyfulness to it."

"I don't disagree with you there," he agreed. "I get it though. It's new. It's different, and, therefore, in a way, it's also scary, but it doesn't have to be freaky scary."

"No, not at all," she replied immediately. "I guess it's just ..." Then she stopped.

"Just?" he asked, waiting for her to complete that sentence. "Is it just that it's so new, so different, that you're hesitant to trust it?"

She glanced over at him and then nodded. "Maybe. I'm not sure it's about trust necessarily. Finding a true friend right now is huge."

"Agreed," he murmured. "I think friendship at this particular stage of our lives is very important, and whatever comes after this, we'll just keep an open mind. How's that?"

At that moment, Shelby raced toward him, carrying a big stick. Laughing, Declan picked up the stick and threw it for her.

"She's so happy now. I mean, she seemed happy before," Carly clarified, "but something's different now, almost a sense of being settled."

"That's good." Declan nodded. "As a War Dog, she hasn't always had an easy time of it, so I'd like to see all of that and more for her. She deserves it."

"Me too," she agreed, with a smile. "You're very good with her."

"I love dogs. Actually I love all animals. I can't say that it will be just dogs in my world."

"Good. I mean obviously I like dogs because I work with them constantly, but—"

"Are you ready to go back to work tomorrow?"

She nodded. "Yes. I need to see a couple kids at a children's center, and tomorrow would be my regular day for seniors, and I know how much they look forward to it."

"So, would you mind if I came with you?"

She looked at him in surprise. "No, but why would you?"

"I don't know. Maybe I'd like to see the kind of work you do, the impact you have on people," he explained. "I was hurt pretty badly and spent a lot of time in military hospitals, then in rehab. There weren't any animals where I was, and looking back it would have been a really good thing. Especially being such an animal lover."

"I'm surprised there wasn't anything there."

"Well, my initial injury was a while ago, and the hospital was just a steady stream of guys like me. Maybe it just didn't occur to anybody at the time. So, it makes more sense if you think about it from that perspective."

"I don't know," she hedged. "Some of this stuff just seems natural to me, but, for a lot of people, things are a little more complicated."

At that, he burst out laughing. "I think everybody makes things more complicated. It's just human nature."

"That's true." She turned to him. "Any thoughts about what you want to do with your life?"

He chuckled at that. "Nothing solid. I'm still looking at options. Maybe that's one of the reasons I would like to see the work that you do."

"Would you ever go into something like this?" she asked curiously, quite surprised. "You seem like more of an action-oriented person."

"I have all kinds of options, based on my previous military years," he shared. "I have dog training experience. I ran a search and rescue dog team for years."

"Oh, wow, really? … Like a K9 unit?"

"That's one avenue, if the War Dog has that kind of training." He looked down at Shelby.

"Are you thinking of Shelby?" she asked, with a note of fear in her voice.

He looked over at her in surprise. "You really care about her, don't you?"

"I do," she admitted, then shrugged. "But honestly, if she has a good home, with somebody who would look after her and love her, I'd be okay with that too. It would be hard to leave her, but it's obvious that she's quite bonded to you."

"Why don't we worry about that later," he said, with a knowing smile. "I think Shelby has a lot of potential that she hasn't been challenged to do yet, and it might be good for her. Some of the War Dogs come back to retire, and they settle in fine with being couch potatoes, but lots of them need more interaction. Keeping them working in some capacity is one way of doing that. They need that constant challenge in order to have a fulfilled life. So it's something we could take a look at."

She nodded. "Rescue dogs will be interesting," she noted, "but it could also be difficult emotionally."

He picked up her hand again and squeezed her fingers. "I was thinking the same thing about your job. I don't imagine that it is any easier at times."

"No," she agreed, "it isn't. That's a good point. I go there one day and think somebody is doing really, really well, only to go back the next to find out they've had a relapse, and I can't see them—or worse, that they're no longer with us. ... Those days are very difficult. You would think I would get wise to it, but it seems to catch me by surprise every time."

"Part of that is probably a bit of denial on your part because that makes it easier to get through the day and to do what you need to do."

"I get that too," she muttered, then sighed. "Some days it's good. Some days? ... I just wonder what I'm doing."

"Do you come out in tears sometimes?"

"Of course. How can you not when you see kids who

shouldn't be in a hospital, much less struggling for life? Sometimes struggling just to breathe and to exist, but instead everything hurts, and so much pain is involved. You wonder at the quality of their lives. And, for some, their time is waning, and that is very hard. Anything I can do to get them a little bit of joy for a few moments and for their parents to see them smile makes me feel better too. However, I don't want to do it simply because it makes me feel better. ... I want to do it for them."

"I suspect it's good for everybody," Declan noted. "When you can give them a bit of joy, I'm sure that helps, and even when you aren't allowed in, the memory of it helps all of you. Anything that eases their pain, while knowing they are not here for very long, makes it easier for you to keep helping others."

"We'll see how you feel about it tomorrow." And, with that, she was reminded of her world, where she was often emotionally attached to some of the patients. It could be a problem and was something she had to let go of to some degree. She could only go there for so long without being impacted, yet it also made it that much harder.

It was a bit easier with the elderly people. At least she felt a sense of completion, a sense of a time coming to an end, with a sense of joy as well because she could make their last few days more comfortable. But the children? No matter what she did, working with the children, while joyful, was very, very hard.

AS CARLY LED the way into the first center the next morning, she had Milly and Daniel with her. Daniel was a dachshund; Milly was a mutt mix. Carly had no clue what Milly was, but her personality was absolutely perfect for the patients. As she walked into the first hospital room, Milly started to get excited.

The older woman in the bed recognized her and immediately called her up onto the bed.

Milly looked back at Carly, who, instead of letting her jump, reached down and lifted her onto the bed. "Hi, Agatha. How are you doing today?"

"I'm doing fine," Agatha replied. "I'm so glad to see you. I was afraid I would miss out."

"Oh my, no," Carly replied. "I might have to miss a day here or there, depending on other jobs and responsibilities, but I do my best to get here."

"Oh, I know that, dear." Agatha smiled. "I meant that my time is coming."

Now Agatha had mentioned things like that before. It was something that happened quite often with Carly's elderly patients, making comments along the same line, which always made Carly pause. "Well, when it is your time, then I hope you have an easy trip," she replied.

"That's the trick, isn't it?" Agatha laughed. "To make the last journey as painless as possible." After she cuddled Milly for a while, she asked Carly, "When you go out, tell the nurse I need to see her, will you?"

"Absolutely." Saying goodbye, Carly gathered up Milly and walked out to the hallway. Knowing that Declan was carefully observing and taking note of every step Carly made, she contacted one of the nurses and told her that Agatha was looking for assistance.

The nurse nodded. "Her time is coming," she stated, with a gentle smile. "She won't be with us much longer now." And, with that, the nurse disappeared down the hallway.

Carly went on to see Jeffry, an older gentleman, who was in the hospital with a heart condition.

When Jeffry looked at her and saw the animals, he immediately smiled. "I'm supposed to be released to go home in a day or two. So I was thinking about my time here, and one of the things I'll miss is my visits with these guys."

"Well, once you get out of this place," Carly replied, with a laugh, "you are free to go visit all kinds of animals."

"Maybe," he said.

She reached down and picked up Daniel, who she knew had a special liking for this gentleman. The two of them had a wonderful visit and cuddled for a time, while Carly just stayed quiet. He looked up at her. "I'm sure it can't be easy to take all this on in the midst of your day, but you really are doing all of us a wonderful service."

She smiled. "I'm glad to hear that. It certainly makes it easier on me knowing that you enjoy seeing these guys."

"Absolutely," he stated.

She stayed for about fifteen minutes and then said goodbye to Jeffry and moved Daniel out and back down the hallway.

The nurse outside motioned to her. "We've got a couple new patients." She quickly provided a rundown.

"How's Jeffry doing?" Carly asked the nurse, as they walked on down the hall. "He told me that he's getting released soon."

The nurse snorted. "Well, that would be nice, but he isn't. He'll likely be here until the end. He keeps coding on us, so we can't let him go at this point."

"Ah, crap," Carly whispered.

"It is what it is, and, at some point in time, we can't bring him back, and that will be the end of it."

"It's still hard though."

"It is, indeed, but, at least here, he's not alone."

Then the nurse led Carly down to the next patient, and that's pretty much how the day went. From one to the next, to the next, until she and Declan and the two dogs came outside into the sunshine. "Well, what do you think?" she asked Declan.

"I think you provide a huge service, and the fact that you can even do this shows what a special person you are."

She raised her eyebrows at that praise.

Declan admitted, "I'm not sure I could even do it. I'd want to scoop everybody up and take them home and protect them."

"Yet we can't," she noted.

"I know, and I get that, but it doesn't mean I have to like it though."

At that, she burst out laughing. "No, generally we don't like having our wishes thwarted. So, if you thought that was an interesting place, the next stop is the children, and I find that much harder."

"*Great*," he muttered. "Do you get through that one with dry eyes?"

"Sometimes," she said, then looked at him with a sheepish smile, "but not very often."

He nodded. "Yeah, that's what I was thinking, but we'll see." By the time they finished going through the children's center, and the two dogs got to visit with several more patients, Carly walked out into the parking lot and stood by the vehicle for a long moment.

He walked up and wrapped an arm around her shoulders. "You okay?"

She smiled at him. "I am. It's just that these kids always hit me so hard."

"I think they're supposed to hit us hard," he shared. "I think we're supposed to see it as a reminder of what we need to live for, plus as an affirmation of why we do what we do. In your case, what you do isn't easy at all. I'll confess I had no idea how emotionally draining something like this would be."

"I don't think there's a choice. Not if you care about people." She gave him a weary smile. "When you think about it, every one of these people is impacted in some way, and we're touching their lives." At that, she opened up the truck door and put the two dogs inside. "That's what I have to remember, so I can make sure that my touch is gentle, light, happy, and full of love."

And, with that, she got into the vehicle. Once Declan was in the driver's seat, she turned her head toward him. "Now I really need to go home. I'm always incredibly overwrought after a few hours with the children."

"Have you ever considered not coming here and sticking with the old folks?"

She nodded. "Yeah, actually I've stopped before, but, in the end, I felt way worse." She sighed. "Look at what they are enduring. If I can brighten their day, give them a few minutes of joy, and let their parents and caregivers see them smile, how can I not?"

"Absolutely. It's obviously a highlight for them." He started the truck and drove away. "How about we go out for lunch?"

"That's a good idea, except we do have the dogs with us. Honestly, would you mind if we just went home?" She sniffed back her tears. "Surely there must still be food at home, and we can have a bite there."

"Okay, and, if not, we could always order in or run to the store." Declan glanced at her, with a worried expression.

She smiled at him. "I'm fine, honest."

"Oh, you're better than fine," he corrected her. "You're fantastic." On that note he drove home, leaving her to stare at him, wondering what on earth was building between them, yet so grateful that something was.

ONCE DECLAN AND Carly and the two dogs were home, Declan quickly walked into the house and checked his phone. He'd had it off the whole time they were visiting patients, even on the drive home. He hadn't considered anything on his phone needed more attention than his experience of sharing a day with Carly at work. He had been overwhelmed by the process she went through on a regular basis. He wasn't sure he had that in him.

He wasn't certain he could handle that kind of emotional aftermath. She also appeared to be fairly emotional at the moment. He put on some coffee, checked in the fridge for food, and called out, "I'll have to run out later today and get some things."

"I can also go shopping," she offered, as she stepped into the kitchen. "I'm not an invalid any more."

He looked over at her, then smiled. "No, you sure aren't. I guess I'm just trying to make myself useful."

"You've been very useful so far"—she smiled—"but, hey, if you want to do the shopping, I could stay and work with the dogs."

"How do they handle it?" he asked, looking at them. "Do they need anything to help them after these visits?"

"Not the way I do, no. Though, if you want to do search and rescue work, that could have a different effect on the dogs. Plus, working with a War Dog, she might react to certain conditions, considering prior service trauma."

He nodded. "I did know one search and rescue dog that needed a teddy bear at the end of a long day, particularly if he found a lot of human remains."

"We often don't give animals the same amount of attention for something like that," she noted. "Yet it can be very hard on them. These guys"—she motioned to Daniel and Milly, who were busy jumping around with the others right now—"do fine. They are more than happy to go visit at the hospital, and they don't seem to be as negatively affected as they could be."

"That's good to hear," Declan said.

"Absolutely. It's hard enough without having a therapy dog emotionally affected as well. Now Fancy, my little teacup dog, she would be overwrought seeing the children. That's why she stayed home today."

"I think it would be tough, really tough. Maybe those emotionally overwrought dogs are the dogs who aren't well suited for therapy." He looked down at Shelby.

"I guess that's the trick, isn't it? Finding out what the dog's temperament is and finding activities to match."

"I've asked for Shelby's training and service records, but I haven't got anything yet."

"That would be interesting to see," she noted. "It could be anything, I suppose."

"It could be, and it could be a lot of different things. These War Dogs are different from a lot of the stateside working dogs. Often they go through multiple layers of training, so they can adapt to a variety of situations. So the same War Dog could be working on finding mines, security, tracking down infidels, and more. There are many different aspects to this."

"Right." Carly looked around and asked, "How about a sandwich?"

"That works." He went ahead and let her change the subject without objection, realizing that she appeared to be more emotionally caught up with Shelby than Carly was willing to let on. But he also knew that Shelby wasn't likely to be part of Carly's therapy work but might need more of a job than what Carly had to offer.

She did seem to be a little bit more willing to open up to the notion of Shelby being with somebody else. The problem was, he wasn't set up and didn't even have a place yet or an idea of what he wanted to do. For him to even consider Shelby and what that might mean in his world was a whole different story.

"If you were to take Shelby and set up something like that, where would you do that?" Carly asked him.

"I was just thinking about that. I mean, it's not as if I even have a true home base right now."

"Where were you originally?"

"Colorado, but that was a long time ago. After the accident, everything went into storage, while I was transferred around the various medical and rehab centers," he shared with her. "It's basically all just sitting there, while I decide what to do."

"I often wondered about that whole storage thing," she said. "I contemplated it myself, while thinking about what I could do with my parents' stuff, but it just ended up becoming a long-term money drain of other people's things. And now, of course, I can't keep my mind on anything but the fact that Henry may not have even been my biological father."

At that, Declan squeezed her shoulder. "We'll leave that topic for now. We did what we could. We submitted your blood sample to be DNA tested. All we can do now is wait for the results. Remember?"

She tossed him a look. "Yeah. So much easier said than done."

He nodded. "I get that. I really do. We'll do the best we can in the meantime, and then we'll move on and find more answers another way," he stated calmly. When she laughed at him, he asked in mock confusion, "What's that for?"

"It's just you, always with an answer for everything."

"There *is* always an answer for everything. We just don't always like it though."

She winced. "So many times, I don't see the things that I don't like. In the past, I've always tended to go straight into turtle mode. Then I would try harder in the opposite direction, generally overdoing in that area as well."

"So maybe you need to stop trying quite so hard either way you go," he offered.

She looked over at him. "It feels too quiet around here."

He slowly put down his coffee cup, as he studied her. "It could be like this for a while, you know?"

She took a deep breath. "I can't say that makes me very happy."

"Just because we want something to happen doesn't mean it will."

"I get it. I really do, but the waiting to see what this asshole will do next is not easy."

He smiled at her. "No, it definitely isn't easy."

"How can you stand it?" she exclaimed. "Being a man of action and all?"

"Practice." He shrugged. "Yes, it's painful at first. Then you realize how much time you waste on counterproductive worry. So you train yourself to focus on productive work, even while waiting."

DECLAN WATCHED CARLY over the next few days, as a pattern was established. On the outside, she appeared calm, controlled, even happy. As they went about their days, as he followed her from job to job through the hospitals and the children's medical centers, she nearly always worked with the dogs in the backyard afterward. He carefully watched everything.

He even worked with Shelby quite a bit to see what she could do and was pleasantly surprised to see how much of her military training she had retained and how well she bonded with him. About four days later he realized that a storm was about to break. He caught Carly outside on the deck, just staring. He walked up and placed a gentle hand on her shoulder. "It's late. Are you ready for dinner?"

She took a shaky breath, and he almost heard it rattling in her chest.

"Tough day, *huh*?"

"Yep, but right now they're all getting to be tough." She held up her hand, and he noted the fine tremor.

"Is that from the work you did today or because of"—he waved a hand around at the property—"all this?"

"It's because of *all this*," she stated, clenching her hands into fists. "I thought I'd be doing better at this point, but I'm sick of all this waiting."

"It's actually harder to do better long-term," he noted. "You can put a lid on all the fears and the frustrations for the moment. Then you go about doing everything that you know to do, but it's still a waiting game."

"A horrible waiting game," she cried out, turning to look at him. "And we don't even know if this guy is out there." She pointed at her land beyond the fence. "I mean, what if he saw I had nothing and took off? Maybe it was a random break-in. Maybe we're just blowing this up, and it's really not a problem at all."

"If that's the case," he replied, squeezing her shoulder before letting his hand fall away, "why are you so nervous?"

She blinked at him. "Instincts."

He nodded. "And you need to listen to them. And let Shelby do her thing too. We can't drop our guard."

Hearing her name, Shelby trotted up to lay her head in Carly's lap. Carly petted the dog, more to soothe herself than anything, he figured. "When I feel as if I dropped my guard, I suddenly remember and freak out because I had a break-in. Maybe somebody's after me. Maybe he isn't." She rolled her eyes and raised her hands in frustration. "I talk myself both in and out of trouble constantly. I just don't get it."

"We'll get a handle on it."

"Imagine if this were to go on for a very long time," she suggested. "I would be a basket case."

"Is this what you already went through with your parents?"

She hesitated, then slowly nodded. "And maybe that's the worst thing," she muttered. "That sense of waiting and knowing there just are no answers." She wrapped her arms around her chest, as if suddenly chilled.

Declan ran his hands up and down her arms to warm her up. "I can't help you with all of it," Declan admitted, "but what I can tell you is that we should be getting the DNA back soon. None of the names that Dean gave us led to anything important. So, until we get more answers, not really a whole lot of threads left to tug. But those we do have *are* still being tugged."

"We haven't even heard from the detective," she added.

"Larry reached out to me just a couple days ago."

"A couple days ago?" she repeated, with a hard snort. "Like that's a help."

He chuckled. "It is a help, just not enough of a help to put your mind at ease."

"No, of course not. I mean, I had a break-in. We had a pop can." She sighed. "Everything is little bits and pieces that actually just make me sound paranoid, and that's the last thing I need. I went through hell over that with my parents. Every time I talked to the shrink, I felt like I was making up some sort of incident to justify the panic going on around me. At one point in time, I just wanted to stop going because I didn't think she believed me."

"If that were the case, she was the wrong therapist for you," he noted.

Carly grimaced, then explained, "She was an old family friend in the field and had worked with my parents a lot. ... She knew everything about it and was potentially dealing with her own trauma from losing my mother, who was a good friend."

"Interesting. I guess it was easier to go to her."

Carly nodded. "Of course it was, and I still stay in touch with her. I was actually wondering if I needed to contact her and set up a few sessions online or something, since we don't live in the same state anymore."

"Will she do that?"

"In a heartbeat," Carly said. "I think, in a way, she took an interest in me just because of what happened. It was a connection to my mother, and they were close as they went to school together. ... It's just one more of those layers of friendship, and you don't realize how important they are, until something like this happens, and then you know. She was one of the few people who was there for me."

"How many other people were around at the time?"

She looked over at him and shrugged. "Not many. I lost all my friends at school. They couldn't handle the fact that I was so traumatized. I needed a shrink, so she stepped up, and I used her services for a long time. Dean wasn't in the picture, of course, having already gone to prison. Nobody was there really. I mean, I had a realtor help me sell the house. And my shrink really helped me to get organized and to find people to arrange the cleaning out and getting rid of the things I didn't want to keep, selling off a bit of the personal stuff that needed to be sold, accessing the safe deposit box, all that kind of stuff."

"Whoa, whoa, whoa." He turned to stare at her. "What was in the safe deposit box?"

She frowned at him. "Oh. ... Documents of some sort."

He let out his breath. "What kind of documents?"

"I don't even know. She just told me to hang on to everything, until I was in a better position to deal with things. I guess all this time I never thought I'd gotten there."

"How about now?" he asked, pressing a little harder. "Because if anything in those documents is important, we need them now."

She blinked. "I don't think so. They were just about my mother's military life—her career, her certificates, and related items."

"Most people don't put that kind of thing in a safe deposit box."

"Oh, it was my parents' box, not just hers, but she was the one who handled it. I can't imagine there would be anything in relation to my paternity." Carly shrugged. "That was hardly something she would want Henry to necessarily see."

"Unless of course he *did* see it, and that's what precipitated all this."

Carly swallowed. "That takes us back down a path that's really ugly and something I don't even want to contemplate."

"Sticking your head in the sand hasn't worked that well so far, has it? So how about now?" She glared at him, and he just smiled. "Where's the safe deposit box?"

"At the bank."

"Well, that's where they typically are, yes," he replied patiently. "A local bank? Is there any way we can check it out?"

"I guess. I suppose I need to, don't I?"

He nodded. "If we're busy cleaning things out of your attic and helping you to deal with that stuff, it's a good time to do the bank box as well, regardless of what we find. It will also put my mind to rest that nothing there pertains to what's currently going on."

"I didn't even think about it, honestly," she muttered. "I'd quite put it out of my mind. I just pay the bill every year and haven't even contemplated what I need to do with the stuff. It's supposed to be something I deal with when I'm ready, except, well, I'm never ready." Then she scrubbed her face with her hands and blew out a long exhale. "Okay, so tomorrow we'll go to the safe deposit box and take a look."

"That'll be good," he said. "Now, how about some dinner?"

She nodded, then looked over at him. "What will I do when you leave? I haven't had to cook for several weeks."

"I've hardly been here that long," he protested, "and, anytime you want to cook, feel free. I'm a bigger eater than you, and food is important to me, so I'm always looking out at least one meal ahead."

"Some people might say you have a problem," she replied in a teasing voice.

He flashed his potent grin at her. "Maybe so, but the problem in my world is making sure I have enough food."

She rolled her eyes at that. "All we do is work, eat, and buy food."

"We cook too," he added, "and get the odd walk in. Come on inside. We'll get some dinner and then an early night for you. Tomorrow is likely to trigger a bit more than what you'll want triggered, and we need to be emotionally stable for it. So we'll get you a good meal and some good sleep."

"You mean, *I* need to be stable," she clarified in a dry tone, but still she let him take her inside, where he started a quick dinner.

CHAPTER 9

CARLY WOKE UP the next morning, with a horrible sense of dread inside. The safe deposit box discussion had kicked in a whole new level of anxiety. She lay here, doing the deep breathing exercises that her shrink had given her years ago. She hadn't had to use it for some time, not until this whole scenario had come up again. Then she got up, had a quick shower, and headed downstairs, not surprised that, no matter how early she got up, Declan was always there ahead of her, and the coffee was always made.

"You are the perfect house guest," she murmured. "Not only do you cook and do dishes, but you're up ahead of me, and I never have to make my own coffee."

He grinned at her. "Hey, I aim to please. I'm very aware that I'm imposing on you."

She frowned at him. "Seriously? I mean, with everything that you do? You're hardly imposing. Besides, you're the one who's keeping an eye out and keeping me safe. I feel like I should be paying you."

He immediately shook his head. "That is not what I want you to feel at all. That's the last thing I want."

"Maybe so, but you're doing an awful lot for me. I plan to pay for the security equipment, but you're the one who installed it," she noted. "Though I haven't even checked it." She stopped, stared at him. "I should though, shouldn't I?"

"Yes. You need to get familiar with it, so you'll remember how to access it and can see it for yourself, whenever you need to."

With that, she walked over to where he had it set up and checked the video on it.

"We can also put that on your phone, if you want."

"That would be a good idea," she said. "Then I can do it every morning."

"That would make for an excellent habit."

As he walked her through the process, she noted, "Every morning it would make me feel better to see that there's been no disturbances during the night."

"Exactly. That alone should be worth your effort."

Vowing to do better and to not leave so much left to him, she looked around the kitchen and asked, "Have you eaten already?"

"No, I was waiting for you," he said cheerfully.

"Good, how about pancakes? I'll make them," she offered, heading to the cupboard and pulling out the supplies she needed. She was a decent cook and felt bad that he had been doing so much of the cooking, while she had been slacking off. Determined to do better, she quickly whipped up a batch of pancakes, making twice as much as she thought she needed because it was him, then added scrambled eggs on the side.

As they ate, he said, "The bank should be open by nine."

She nodded. "Yes, so I figured we can get there just after that."

"Good."

"Don't worry. I haven't changed my mind."

"That's good. We never really know what we might find."

"After I moved here several years ago, which involved transferring over the bank box contents, I told the detective about it. I thought the police would check, but I don't know if they ever did."

"The local cops handling your parents' murders?"

She nodded, then frowned, as she thought about it. "I don't know what they did or didn't do. I guess we can't really get a hold of the case file."

"I've seen what I'm allowed to see. Badger sent it to me."

She stopped, put her fork down, and asked, "Do I get to see it?"

He immediately shook his head. "Hell no you don't. That's the last thing you need to look at."

She winced, then picked up her fork and continued eating. "I guess it's got the crime scene photos and all that, right?"

"It has a lot of stuff in it, and a lot of stuff that's pretty useless. The door was opened without the use of force, meaning that they let somebody in, which I was expecting, knowing they weren't that concerned about security."

"Maybe she didn't even bother locking it."

"Yet you say *she* …"

Carly eyed him, quiet for a moment. "My father was very forgetful and really not on the ball when it came to that kind of stuff, so that would have fallen to Mom. However, if she was really tired, she easily could have forgotten."

"Which is too bad because a simple security system can make all the difference."

"It can," she hedged, "but it can also make no difference at all." And, with that cryptic tone, she finished the food on her plate, then got up and loaded the dishwasher. He quickly joined her. By the time the kitchen was cleaned up, she checked her watch and nodded. "If we leave now, we should get right in." She looked down at the dogs, then frowned. "I guess we should leave everybody here."

"Yeah, we won't be long." Taking a deep breath, he grabbed her hands.

She looked down to see that both were in hard little fists. "I hadn't realized just how difficult this would be. Yet, after everything else, I don't know why."

"That's important too, you know? We need to see just what triggers this kind of upset for you. Did something happen the last time you were at the safe deposit box?"

She frowned and shook her head. "No, nothing happened at all. I didn't even really look at anything, once I saw there wasn't any money, jewelry, or weapons," she added, with half a chuckle. "Then I just put everything into an envelope. The realtor people were helping me organize everything, told me that if it was important enough to keep in a safe deposit box, I should just rent one wherever I ended up. So, that's what I did."

"Well, that was smart in a sense, but it would have been good if you at least had the mind-set to take a quick look to confirm if anything important was in there."

"What was important to me at that time was the fact that my parents were dead, murdered, and they were never coming back. Whatever was in that safe deposit box was theirs, not mine, and that alone was hard enough." She felt the tears forming in the back of her eyes. She brushed them away impatiently. "I need to do this. I hadn't even realized it would be so difficult."

He didn't say anything more and just took her hand and led the way outside. When they got to their vehicles, he said, "Let's take mine."

She nodded. "Is that just in case I break down and can't drive home?"

"Look. If you break down, don't worry about it. It's normal and to be expected really, so you don't need to feel bad about it."

"Too late," she replied, then laughed. "I really do think I may need to call my doctor and see about booking a couple sessions. Maybe just something to help me through this last bit."

"Considering the time frame that's gone by, it's probably a good idea. I don't think that there's any moratorium on grief though."

Grateful for his understanding, she got into the truck with him and gave him directions on how to get to the bank.

When he drove a different way, she said, "You didn't even need my help, did you?"

"I'd already looked it up on Google. Plus I didn't want to take the same pathway we may have taken before."

She froze at that. "Right. See? I'm so focused on the safe deposit box now that I wasn't even thinking about our regular problems."

"And that's not something you need to worry about today. Let me do the worrying."

Then she sank back and relaxed ever-so-slightly. "Have I told you how grateful I am that you're here?" she whispered.

"I get it." He gave her a warm, understanding smile. "You're welcome."

DECLAN PARKED BEHIND the bank. He got out, waited for her, and, with an arm around her shoulders, asked, "How are you holding up?"

She shrugged. "I'll just be glad when it's over."

He nodded and led the way into the center of the bank, his gaze ever watchful. So far, she hadn't picked up on the fact that he was taking different routes every time they went out. It wouldn't necessarily stop anybody who was following them when they ran these errands, but it might throw them off a time or two. Plus, every time they went for a walk at night, he always guided her in an almost circular route around her property to confirm nobody was there.

Twice he thought he'd caught somebody sitting and waiting, but, when he'd gone back out later with the dogs, the person had been gone. He'd also sent the description of the vehicle he saw once to Badger, but it wasn't enough to get an ID because Declan couldn't get any license plate numbers. But he'd never let up his guard, and he knew Shelby had never let up hers.

The War Dog was always there, always around and close by, waiting for instruction. It's partly what Carly had seen as being a bond between her and Declan. However, it was more about Shelby working. Carly just didn't know it, and Shelby was quite happy to have something to do. He'd left her on guard at home, but right now he had to look after Carly, as she faced yet another emotional pitfall in the road of her life.

It wasn't that she couldn't have handled one of these on her own. It was that she was dealing with more than one simultaneously. And they just seemed to keep coming.

As they stepped forward to be served, Carly told the clerk that she needed access to her safe deposit box. With that, they were led into a small room within the vault area. She handed over the keys, and, while they waited, they were led into a cubicle, and the bank box was brought to them.

When it was left in front of them, and the bank clerk had gone, Declan looked down at it, then at her. She seemed frozen.

"I'm scared to open it," she murmured.

"Do you want me to?" he offered.

She looked over at him, then squared her shoulders with that same sense of determination she used to handle her own business. "No, I'll do it." She reached down, turned the key, and popped the lid back. Inside was the envelope she had put in it. Nothing else. She stared at it. "I don't know why it's such a letdown, since I'm the one who put this in here." She gave a nervous laugh. "Lord, I'm just … it's all starting to get to me."

"And that's fine," he reassured her. He reached in, picked up the envelope, and asked, "May I look?"

She nodded.

He took the envelope and dumped the contents onto the big table and noted it was mostly papers. He flipped through them, seeing some printouts, banking accounts, and what looked like copies of certifications and trainings that her mom had obviously felt were important.

When he got to the end of the stack, he found one small laminated plastic card. He looked at it and slowly whistled.

"What is it?" she asked, peering over at him. "I don't remember seeing that."

"It was stuck in between a couple documents, so, unless you had actually been looking at what everything was, it's small enough that you might not have seen it."

She studied it, frowning. "Actually I kind of do remember, but I didn't know what it was."

"It's a DNA test, laminated for safekeeping."

"*Great*. Whose it is?"

"Yours and your father's."

She looked at him in surprise. "You mean Henry's?"

He nodded. "Yes, and, in this case, Henry is not the man you thought he was."

"Okay, so what do you mean by that? Meaning he isn't my biological father?"

"No, he was not. The man you called *Dad* is not your biological father. We still don't know who is yet. This card doesn't tell us that, but it does say that it's not Henry, and his DNA test is here." Declan took a picture of the DNA card, then flipped through the rest of the documents. "Let's take all this home, and you can either retain your safe deposit box rental if you want, or you can let the box rental slide."

"I think there's still quite a few months left that's paid for."

"Good, in that case, just leave everything as it is. You'll have it available if you need it, and you can always think about what you want to do with that later, after we have gone through these docs."

She nodded. And, with that, they stepped out to tell the clerk that they were done. Then he walked outside, with Carly ever-so-slightly behind him. As he studied the area, finally like a triggered response, he saw what he expected.

"What is it you see?" she asked at his side.

"Hopefully nothing," he murmured, "but I've already sent off the photos of the two DNA test results to Badger, and we'll see what comes back." He led the way to his truck and then drove to the grocery store, where they picked up a few more groceries.

Finally, in the grocery store, she stopped and glared at him. "That's it. We need to go home," she declared.

He looked at her in surprise. "Why?"

"You're making me even more nervous. You're constantly searching and hunting around, as if you're expecting to be followed."

He reached up a gentle hand, stroked her cheek, and replied, "We were followed."

CHAPTER 10

ONCE THEY WERE home again, Carly moved like an automaton. She knew it was stupid, but to have Declan confirm her fears in the grocery store and then hustle her through the cashier and back out to the truck, all made her beyond nervous. Once she got into the kitchen to put away the groceries, she managed to do it without breaking anything, even as she slammed items from one end to the other, as they needed to go. Finally she turned to confront him. "When were you going to tell me?"

"Not this way and not this fast," he replied. "I was hoping to find out who it was first because more information without answers or clarity wouldn't help you."

She took a deep breath. "Still, it feels a bit like a betrayal."

He stared at her in surprise. "Why?"

She frowned. "I'm not sure. I'll have to think about it."

"You do that, and, in the meantime, remember that you are looking for answers, and I didn't have any. I was just trying to get close enough to get them."

"Was I in any danger?"

"We're all in danger if this guy is coming after us. So far, I just felt like we were being tailed. What happens now may be a whole different story."

At that, she immediately asked, "What does that mean?"

"They know we took something out of the safe deposit box," he began. "So, in theory, it'll be whatever it is. If they're looking for something, they'll want it."

"Jesus." She reached up a shaky hand to her heart. "So now what?"

"Well, I took photos of the DNA test and sent them off, as I told you. As for the rest of the stuff, I suggest that, if it's important, we scan and photocopy it. That way, you'll have copies in a digital format as well."

"Fine." She grabbed the envelope, headed to her office, and methodically scanned all the documents that came out of the safe deposit box. "I should have done this in the first place," she muttered.

"Maybe, but, if you didn't think it was important, you wouldn't have."

"It's not even that. I didn't give it a thought. I just wanted it all to go away, to be something I didn't have to deal with."

"I can't blame you for that."

She shrugged. "I'm just disgusted that I'm back in the same scenario but way worse. If somebody wants this information, what am I supposed to do with it? Post it on my mailbox and say 'Here. Just take it?'"

He looked at her in surprise and then laughed. "You know what? That's not a bad idea."

She stared at him in shock. "Seriously?"

"Well, at least he'll know that we caught him and that we're on to him. And, if he wants it, he *can* take it," Declan stated calmly.

She snorted, then grabbed the envelope, stuffed inside all the originals, except for the DNA card, and wrote on the front, *Just take the damn thing*. Then promptly propped it up on a chair on her front porch. "I doubt that he'll come and get it, or, even if he does, that it'll be what he wants. I don't understand the DNA records, outside of the fact that apparently Henry was not my biological father," she muttered bitterly, "and I dearly wish my mother was around to explain that because this is just BS."

"Yet you're not the only one to have found out after the fact."

"No, of course not, but, at the same time, not everybody's parents were murdered, not everybody's parents are gone to the point where I can't get answers from them."

"No, you can't." At that, his phone rang.

She glanced down at it and said, "I'll go put on some coffee."

DECLAN DIDN'T SAY anything because they'd already had quite a bit of coffee, but, if that kept her going, he wouldn't stop her. When he checked his Caller ID, the phone call was from Dean. "Hey, Dean. What's up? Have you heard anything?"

"No, I haven't heard very much at the moment. What about you?"

"No, I checked out all your friends," he replied, listening to Dean's almost querulous questions on the other end. "I would like some clarity though, on your relationship with Susan, Carly's mother."

At that came silence on the other end.

Declan announced, "I'm putting you on Speaker."

Carly turned and looked at Declan in shock but managed to say, "Hey, Dean. I'm here."

Dean asked, "What exactly do you mean by clarity on our relationship?" While he may have regained his senses, his voice was a little shaky.

Carly spoke up. "I've just found out that Henry was not my father by blood."

A shocked gasp came from the other end. "No. What do you mean?"

"I think you know what I mean," she said, her voice gentle. "I guess the question that I'm still waiting to find out is whether or not you're my father." At that, the older man burst into tears and sobbed through the phone. She reached up a hand to her mouth. When he finally calmed down, she whispered, "Does that mean you are?"

"I don't know. I knew she was pregnant, and I knew it was a possibility, but I didn't know for sure."

"What kind of relationship did my parents have that this was even a possibility?" she cried out. "And, of course, neither of them are here for me to talk to."

"I know, and I'm so sorry for what you've been through."

"What we need now," Declan added, "is honesty. We need to know what happened because Carly's still in danger."

"Still?" Dean cried out. "Oh no. Did getting out of prison trigger all this?"

"Well, if that's true, it's only happened because you're innocent," Declan noted.

"I swear to you," Dean replied, his voice growing in strength, "I *am* innocent. I didn't steal or sell anything. I did none of the things I was charged with."

"And served time for," she reminded him. "The fact is, you have every right to prove your innocence, if you can."

"Well, that's where the problem comes in. I was hoping that somebody would have proof."

"The only thing I found out today was proof that Henry wasn't my biological father," she snapped. "And, right now, there's a hell of a lot of questions I'd like to ask my mother."

"I'm sorry for that," Dean whispered. "I loved her. I loved her so much, and yet she wasn't mine."

"Yet you were touching what wasn't yours," she stated in a harsh voice.

"Yes, you're right," he confirmed, his tone stiff. "After it happened, she went back to your father and told me it was all over. When she found out she was pregnant, I asked her if she knew whose it was. She told me that it was your father's, and I had no option but to believe her," he added. "But I always wondered, until a few days ago. The moment I saw you, I knew for sure."

"I didn't know for sure," Carly cried out. "Actually Declan here suggested that apparently I look like you," she shared, her voice turning soft.

"I'm sorry that you've been hurt, and obviously I'm more than happy to take the test in order to confirm either way."

"You don't need to," Declan noted. "Your DNA is on file, and I pulled a favor to get it tested against hers already."

"Of course, the DNA from my conviction."

"Yes, but we haven't got a result yet."

"No, it can take a bit of time. ... I know things have changed over the years, but some things never did, and what I can tell you is that I loved your mother dearly. I would have done anything to have her leave your father and be with me, but I also knew that she loved him."

"Yet how could she have loved him if she had an affair

with you?" Carly asked.

Dean was silent for a moment. "Because your father did something that caused her to leave him temporarily. He had an affair himself. Susan was so devastated, and I think she only went with me to get back at him."

"Good God, the tangled webs we weave."

"Exactly, and I should have never touched her, but I couldn't resist the opportunity to show her how good we could be. But your father contacted her and apologized. He promised her the other relationship was over and that he would never do it again. She believed him, and honestly, in fairness to him, he was faithful ever after. At least as far as I know."

"Great. I don't suppose you know who it was he had an affair with, do you?" Declan asked.

Dean hesitated. "Maybe, but I'm not certain, and I feel like it would be dishonorable to put that slur on somebody else."

Carly spoke up. "I'm trying to figure out what the hell is going on with my world right now, and I would think you would want to know too."

"Why?"

"Because, if you're innocent, what are the chances that Henry found out that I am yours, and sending you to prison was his way of punishing you?"

He hesitated. "That thought did cross my mind, but we were very good friends."

"Good friends don't touch another man's wife," Declan stated, his voice hard. "I'm not blaming you, but, if Henry found out, it might have been more of a betrayal than he could handle. I don't know what kind of a man he was, but he might have found it hard to walk back from something like that."

"He was a hard man," Dean replied. "A very hard man."

"So," Carly began, "maybe instead of keeping secrets, we should see if anything else needs to be brought out into the open and see if my father set you up for this. And, if that's the case, where did he get the evidence, whose help did he have, and how do we reverse it?"

"I don't know, but I might know who does." And, with that, Dean hung up.

She slowly looked over at Declan. "Now what?"

"We'll have coffee, and we'll sit down and relax a bit. Then I'll phone Badger and see if I can get some help on a different issue."

She glared at him. "No secrets."

He shook his head. "No secrets, but I think it's important that we find out about Dean's case, as to who offered the proof and whether Henry could have manufactured it."

She blanched. "Wow. It's one thing to find out your parents are murdered. It's another thing to find out their marriage was a sham, and it's still another thing to find Henry potentially incriminated an innocent man out of revenge."

Declan nodded. "You can be upset about that all you want, but, for now, why don't we focus on getting to the bottom of it. Then we'll deal with the fallout later, but first we have to know exactly what we're dealing with."

CHAPTER 11

TRUE ENOUGH, AFTER Carly and Declan sat outside with their coffee for a while, he finally spoke.

Declan looked over at her and shared, "I just need a few minutes." He got up and called Badger, walking and pacing, within hearing distance so it wasn't secret, but not on Speakerphone, which she could understand.

After a moment or two, she got up to get another cup of coffee. Out of curiosity and seeking a diversion from the phone conversation, she stepped onto the front porch and stared.

She looked all around the porch. *The envelope was gone.* She bolted back out to where Declan was still on the phone and cried out, "The envelope, it's gone." He looked at her in shock and raced forward, but instead of heading out to the front, he went straight to check the security cameras, ending his call on the way. She swore under her breath. She should have done the exact same thing, only faster. It hadn't even occurred to her.

Castigating herself, she followed him, and stood behind his shoulder, so she could see what was there. And sure enough, the image of a tall slim man approached the porch, dressed all in black, wearing a black baseball cap. He came up with a box in his arms, as if to make a delivery, then glancing around, saw the envelope and stared at it for a moment. Pulling the bill of his hat a bit lower, he picked up the envelope, then turned and quickly left. She stared at the screen, dumbfounded. "My God, he actually took it."

"Yeah, and the question is," Declan added, as he took screen shots of the person's face, even though it wasn't a great image, "who is this guy?"

"I don't know."

"It could be the same man that I saw walking away from your house that day," he noted, checking the time stamp, "What I don't like is the fact that he was here literally ten minutes after we put the envelope out there."

"Probably when we went outside or while we were on the phone."

He nodded. "He probably hopped the front yard fence and easily could have heard us talking on the phone, realized we were occupied, and walked right onto the front porch."

"What was in the box he carried though?"

"Probably nothing, or maybe he would leave you something. I don't know. Maybe he was carrying a weapon and planned to come in, but then saw the envelope and decided to take that first." Declan swore. "Hell of a time for me to call my boss."

"And yet maybe that was the call that he heard." She shook her head. "Honestly I'm glad that he came while you were busy. I don't want to deal with him, yet, at the same time, I'm angry and confused. I just want him to sit down and tell me what the hell he wants from me."

At that, a man spoke up behind her. "That's fine. We can do it that way too."

She turned around, shocked to see the same man they were looking at on the security camera, but standing here in her home, with a gun in his hand. Shaking her head, she noted that the dogs were out in the backyard, even Shelby. "What the hell do you want from me?" she cried out. "I don't even know who you are."

"No, but I know who you are," he stated, with a fat smile. "It's kind of nice to be in the know for a change. It seems like all I've done is chase you around for quite a long time now."

She stared at him. "Please tell me that you're not the one who killed my parents."

He looked at her in surprise, then shook his head. "No, I didn't kill your parents, but I sure as hell know who did."

"THERE YOU ARE," Declan gave a nonchalant shrug. "Although I'm not sure why you bothered with the gun this time."

Declan ignored Carly's shocked gasp at his side, just wrapping his arm around her shoulders, tucking her up close. "I presume you got the envelope."

The guy stared at him. "You really did leave it there for me, didn't you?"

"Sure. Just trying to make it easy for you to get it. I mean, you followed us to the bank, and you followed us home again. I figured, what the hell. I might as well make it easy on you and save you all the trouble." Declan motioned at the gun. "Apparently that didn't work."

"Yeah, but what I wanted wasn't in the damn envelope, and you knew that."

"No, I actually don't." Declan frowned at him. "Maybe you should just tell me what you're looking for."

"What did you hold back?"

"DNA," she replied immediately. "The damn DNA card. If you let me go pick it up, I'll bring it to you."

"Where is it?"

She pointed to the counter. He shuffled over to the side, picked up the card, looked at it, and asked, "What the hell does this even mean?"

"Nothing important. I don't know what it is that you think you're looking for, but that's the only other thing that was in the envelope."

"Why didn't you let me have that too then? Obviously it's important."

"It's personal," she replied. "It means that Henry wasn't my biological father."

He looked at her in surprise and then he started to laugh. "Well, that is rich. The bastard did that to you too, did he?"

She stared at him, her jaw dropping. "I'm not sure what you're saying here."

"What I'm saying is that your father, or apparently *not* your father, is actually my father."

At that confession, she studied the gunman, her face crumbling visibly. Declan wrapped his arm tighter around her, pulled her up closer, and just rocked her on the spot.

The gunman continued. "Why the hell should she get everything? I mean, I'm the one who grew up without a father."

She looked over at him from the comfort of Declan's arms. "I get that, and I'm very sorry. I've only just discovered that I grew up without my real father, and I didn't even know until today."

He nodded. "I don't think that makes us siblings though," he declared.

"No, it does not," she confirmed. "Unless we had the same mother."

"No, we sure as hell didn't," he said, with a snort. "Your mom was a capital bitch."

At that, she stiffened. Declan tried to give her a warning hug, but she wasn't having anything to do with it. "Takes a lot of nerve to come into my house, then stand here and spew all these nasty things about my family."

"Your family made my life hell," he snapped. "All I ever wanted was to grow up in a normal family, but no. I wasn't allowed that, all because Henry had you. That's really rich, especially now, considering that you weren't even his. How ironic is that?" The gunman glared at her, as if trying to figure out what this new information meant. "What a mess. What a fucking waste."

"I don't understand. Who is your mother then? If we don't have the same mother, and yet you have my father, then obviously he must have had an affair." Immediately she stopped. "Oh."

"Oh yeah, he did. So, you heard about that, did you?"

"I heard about it today, from the man who potentially *is* my biological father. But I don't actually know whether he is or not. I'm waiting for DNA results on it."

"Well, if you're talking about Dean, he absolutely is your father. Of course you probably want the DNA to cross the *T*s and dot the *I*s, but that won't change anything. That old man went to hell and back, all because of Henry too."

She swallowed hard. Declan looked at her and said, "Look. So far he's just spewing, and it could be all lies for all we know. We don't have to believe anything yet. Unless of course he wants to prove it."

"No, he's right," the gunman agreed, with a casualness

that meant he had something up his sleeve. "You don't have to believe it, but I do have proof though. Plenty of it."

"What kind of proof?"

"The same proof that my mother used to blackmail Henry all these years, so he would at least support us."

She stared at him. "I still don't understand."

"No, of course not. You were never intended to understand any of this. Henry is the one who put Dean in jail. Henry manufactured all the evidence against Dean. They worked in the same department after all, so it was pretty easy for Henry to do. Pretty sure old Dean probably knew what was going on too but felt so damn guilty about having an affair with his best friend's wife that Dean let it happen." The gunman shook his head. "And that's just bullshit too. Henry is a capital *A* asshole."

When Carly shuddered again, Declan faced the gunman. "You might want to remember that she lost her parents in a single event and never had a chance to ask or to get any answers to these questions."

"And that's fine." The gunman sneered. "I never got the chance to get any answers either, and he was my father too. And you can bet I sure as hell wanted to get some."

"You mean about why he wasn't there for you?" Carly asked.

"And why he chose your bitch of a mother over mine. I mean, he'd been having the affair with my mom for years, always promising that he'd leave his wife and marry her. That's apparently the only reason she went ahead and had me," he stated, with an eye roll. "Not that there was a real easy way to get things done back then, but being a doctor, it would have been easier for her."

At that bit of information, Declan felt Carly stiffening in

his arms. He squeezed her gently, offering reassurance. "That's all very interesting," Declan snidely replied, "but it doesn't explain why you're here and what you're after."

"Sure it does. I want all the blackmail material my mother used."

"What good will that do?" Carly sounded quite confused.

Declan looked down at her. "It will implicate his mother," he told her. "That's what he's afraid of. He's afraid something would get his mother in trouble. One question though. Why now?"

"Because Dean is reopening the investigation into his case."

"As he should."

"As he should," the gunman agreed sincerely. "The guy got totally screwed over by his best friend. I mean, I get it, the need for revenge. Dean was screwing his best friend's wife, so maybe the court-martial is a form of justice on its own. But, considering that his so-called best friend was screwing around on the woman Dean loved, maybe not. You know, if they'd just been honest with each other, Henry could have left your mother, and your mother could have spent her life with Dean, and you would have had your biological father, plus I would have had my biological father, and everybody would have been happy," he stated in disgust.

"But, no, Henry decided that he would stay with your mother, and your mother got too righteous and stayed with him instead of leaving him for Dean, and I'm the one who got shafted. Well, and Dean, of course, but nobody gave a shit about him, right? He's one of those honorable people who screwed themselves over after a single mistake."

"What about the sins of your mother?" Carly asked.

"She blackmailed Henry all these years. I had no idea he supported your family at all, much less because he was being blackmailed."

"Well, she kept it to a reasonable amount at least. Did you ever go back and check his bank accounts?"

She shook her head. "No, I never did."

He nodded. "But the thing is, with the reinvestigation into Dean's case, it means they'll take another look. This time, Dean will point them in the right direction, which is to Henry. No way Dean won't do that now. Everybody's gone, and he wants to clear his name before he dies. I think, in his heart of hearts, he was hoping that maybe he could end up with some sort of a relationship with you, since, after all, you are *his* daughter," the gunman noted in a mocking tone.

She took a deep breath. "What, and you're thinking the investigation may have brought up the blackmail payments to your mother?"

"Of course it would have come up. Don't be dense. They can get the history from the banks without any trouble at all these days. They'll need a warrant, sure, but you would hand it over in a heartbeat, wouldn't you?"

She nodded numbly.

"Of course you would." The gunman scowled. "So naturally my mother is not impressed."

"No, of course not. I'm sorry for your mother."

The gunman just stared at her. "Jesus Christ, you really are a complete innocent, aren't you?"

"Look. A lot of people have been hurt already," Carly said in a pleading voice. "Can't we just leave it where it is?"

"But it won't stay where it is, remember? Did you not hear what I just said? Dean has already reopened his case and has formally requested a new look at his trial. He's also handed over some compelling evidence of his innocence, and it does point to Henry. He probably didn't want to tell you that. And, yeah, I followed you to his place too. It seems like all I've done is drive around town on stupid little errands, but today I saw you go into that bank, and I got suspicious because there was just enough nervousness in your actions when you came out and you looked like you were devastated."

She shrugged. "Not so much devastated as shattered. That was when I found the DNA document that confirmed Henry wasn't my biological father." She raised both hands.

"Wow, you really just found out today, *huh*?" The gunman laughed. "That was one of the things that my mother told your father."

"How would she know?" she asked, staring at the gunman, fascinated. "Nobody knew."

"Yeah, somebody did know," the gunman argued, and then he started to laugh hysterically.

When Carly looked up at Declan, he smiled, wondering how long it would take her to connect the dots. She was obviously too dazed by this turn of events to put it all together.

The gunman turned his gaze on her. "Jesus Christ, even now you still don't get it, do you?" He looked at Declan. "Why would you want somebody you can't even have an intelligent conversation with?"

At that, she stiffened. "You don't have to be insulting. I get that something's going on here that I haven't quite figured out, and I'm so sorry if I didn't get there as fast as you think I should have, but that doesn't make me stupid."

"Yeah, it does," he stated, with a negligent shrug of his gun arm. "The thing is, it doesn't matter anyway because, whether you know or not, at this point in time I really can't let you live."

At that, Declan shook his head. "Seriously? You haven't killed anybody yet. Why would you start now?"

Hearing the sound of the dogs barking outside, the gunman added, "I sure hope you have somebody to look after the dogs."

"I don't," Carly snapped, "and they're therapy dogs. They *like* working with people."

"*Huh*, well, maybe I'll take that shepherd. That one really is a fine animal, and I've always wanted a dog like that."

A note of wistfulness filled his tone, and Carly appeared startled.

Declan wasn't startled at all. With a broken home and a family who didn't work the way other families worked, it only made sense that there would be some things in the gunman's life that he had missed out on.

"I'm sorry about your family," she said again.

The gunman shook his head again. "Jesus Christ, you'll never get anywhere in life if you keep apologizing for shit you didn't even do."

"I may not have done it, but apparently my presence was a factor."

He nodded. "It sure was. I'm only older than you by a few weeks, you know? Henry planned to leave your mother when he found out mine was pregnant, right up until he found out that your mother was pregnant too. Then Henry changed his mind. The joke was on him later when Mom told Henry whose kid you really were." The gunman started to laugh again and walked over to the kitchen door, pulled it open, and the dogs came racing in, milling all around. "Good Christ," he said. "How many do you have?"

"Four for therapy and the shepherd. She's already had a pretty rough life."

He looked at her and nodded. "Well, at least you rescue dogs. You can't be all bad."

"I'm not bad at all," she stated, "and having my parents murdered was one of the hardest things in my life." She asked him again, "Did you kill them?"

He looked at her in surprise, shook his head, and said, "No, I didn't. I already told you that. But I know who did."

"I know you said that earlier, but I just wondered if maybe you were lying."

He narrowed his gaze at her. "I'm not a liar," he declared. "Your father Henry was and even your mother. They were liars for sure. Susan passed you off as Henry's child all those years, when you were really Dean's. Susan lied to you your whole life."

"You seem to know so much about my family," she whispered. "So who is your mother?"

The gunman looked at her, then over at Declan. "Have you figured it out?"

Declan nodded. "Yeah, I sure have."

At that, she stared at him, stunned. "What? What am I missing?"

Declan asked, "Who would you have talked to about moving and about cleaning out the house and having to go through it all? Who knows you all too well and everything about your family?"

She looked at him in shock. "Nobody."

"Think again. You've already mentioned her to me."

"Well, no, just my psychologist." Then her gaze widened. She turned and looked at the gunman. "Is Annie your mother?"

At that, he laughed gleefully. "Yeah, she sure is."

Such an affectionate note of admiration filled his tone that Declan realized, for all of what they'd been through, this man still held his mother in high regard.

"Therefore," the gun asked, looking down at her, "who killed your parents?"

"But Annie had no reason to. Dean was in prison, and my parents already knew."

"So, who would have held your heritage against Henry and Susan?"

She let out a long exhale. "Annie, … but I didn't even know about it."

"No, but she also knew Dean, didn't she?" Declan asked the gunman.

The gunman turned to Declan. "Yes, they were all friends back in the day, and, when Annie saw you, she wondered and fussed away at it, until she finally got to the truth of the matter. Once she realized that you were Dean's and that her lover had chosen to stay with an unfaithful wife, raising another man's child rather than being with her and me, well, Annie and Henry had quite a fight over it all, and Henry had some pretty choice words to say to her.

"Annie went over to tell your mother all about it, and that's when things got ugly. Annie ended up killing them both. Your parents were the kind of people who couldn't even imagine that Annie would be like that. But you know? Eighteen years of watching someone else have what you really wanted, all because of some other child who wasn't even Henry's to begin with, just made Annie so angry that she ended up shooting them both and left."

Carly was quiet for a moment, then spoke softly, as it all began to fall into place. "She had the perfect excuse for being there because she had been there many times before, hadn't she?"

He nodded.

"She was actually over a fair bit, which was one of the reasons I went to see her afterward."

"Of course," he noted, "and imagine how that made Annie feel, knowing that she put it all into play. I thought about that and asked if she was ever sorry for what she did to you. Paraphrasing, it was basically, hell no, because you were just the bastard child responsible for Annie not having what she really wanted all those years."

"So, she blamed the child?" Carly asked.

He nodded. "Yes, she blamed you. Maybe not all that fair, but, hey, who cares?"

Declan watched as the gunman stroked the back of the dogs. The little ones at his ankles were sniffing around, running back and forth around the place, but Shelby just sat off to the side, her gaze wary.

Declan had signaled for her to stand guard but to stay quiet. As the gunman walked over to the kitchen counter, he snatched up a leash. "I'll just take the dog while I'm here." Still chuckling at that, he looked over at Declan and said, "Hey, I would have left you alive, and I could have, but, at this point in time, there are just too many problems."

Carly shifted slightly, facing the gunman. "And you can't have your mother kill two people and you not kill two as well, is that it?"

Her voice was stronger than Declan expected.

The gunman looked at her and shrugged. "I don't give a shit about that. I'm way the hell better than my mother anyway. Besides, I sure as hell won't let my seed go fertilize some random field." He snorted. "She should have just dealt with it way back then. I mean, if she was gonna kill your mother anyway, why didn't she do it twenty years ago? She and Henry could have been totally happy, right?" As he went to put the lead on the dog, the gunman glanced back over at Declan. "Is this your dog or hers?"

"It's *my* dog," he stated calmly, and, at that, he gave a sharp hand signal, and Shelby jumped.

CHAPTER 12

CARLY WATCHED IN shock as Shelby—the calmest, gentlest, friendliest overgrown puppy—turned into this ferocious beast that jumped up and latched onto the wrist of the gunman, bringing the gun completely down to the ground, even as his trigger finger went off, firing bullet after bullet into the floor.

But he didn't have time to do anything else, as he was screaming so loud. Declan moved so fast that the gunman had already been dropped to the ground, with his wrist still in Shelby's mouth, growling, ready for round two. It was over shockingly fast, yet gratifying and terrifying to watch at the same time.

"Can you get Shelby to stop?" Carly cried out, hating the sounds of the man's sobbing, with Shelby barking mad.

He nodded. "Get me some zip ties." Surprised, she bolted to the kitchen drawer and pulled out zip ties, along with some straps. He took what he wanted and quickly tied the gunman's wrists and then his ankles. With the gunman secured, he gave the command for Shelby to relax, and she released her grip on the gunman and sat back down.

"Now guard."

Immediately Shelby's attention wavered, her ears went up, and she started to move, just as another bullet flew through the air. Shelby howled, leapt, and took off under the table, as several more bullets peppered behind her.

Screaming, Carly turned and found herself staring at her doctor, Annie. "My God. After all this time, it really was you?"

"Sure it was me."

"You sat there in that office, letting me bawl my eyes out, telling you how devastated I was because of the loss of my parents, and you didn't give a shit for a moment."

"Well, it made me smile on the inside, considering it was all your fault anyway."

"What do you mean it was my fault? I was an innocent child and didn't have anything to do with the mess you adults had made."

"Well, it wasn't me," Annie declared. "All I wanted was the man I loved to care more about me than that bitch he was married to."

That just left Carly gasping.

Annie motioned at Declan, who was checking Shelby. "Get up."

Declan slowly stood.

"Now that the damn bitch of a dog is taken out, I thought you might enjoy the irony of being shot by the same gun that killed your parents. I don't really give a shit if the cops figure out it's the same gun," she admitted. "We're in a completely different state, so they won't even look."

"If they won't look," Carly noted, "I'm sure Dean will make them."

"Dean has his own problems right now, as he is currently bleeding to death on his couch," she said, with a laugh. "No way I'm letting you put my only child in jail like this."

"Yeah, great job raising him, by the way," Declan noted. "So, what will you do, just shoot more of us?"

"Why not? After the first one, it gets easier. You know, over the years, I must have thought of a million different ways to kill your mother," she told Carly. "Yet I kept holding back, always thinking that Henry would change his mind. I started blackmailing him at some point to get some financial support, but I'll be damned when one day he told me that he wouldn't pay anymore. That's when I told him that he wasn't even your father." Annie gleamed with pride.

"God, the look on his face, I loved it. I hadn't even figured it out until I spoke to some of the friends that we had around at the time. I pieced it backward, and I went and saw Dean, actually visited him in the prison. Of course we knew each other way back when, but I saw him again, after you were a bit older, and I realized it was true. So, I made sure that Henry knew about that, and, God, he hated your mother at that moment. That's how he died, you know? Still hating your mom. I thought it was brilliant. Susan was terrified that he would find out and pleaded with me not to do anything to hurt him or you. But I wasn't planning on hurting you then," Annie stated, with a snort. "All I wanted to do was get back at them."

"And now you have a chance to kill us all, is that it?" Carly asked.

"It sure is," Annie said. "Not that it'll make much difference. My son and I will take off. We'll go to another place where we can start fresh."

"How fresh can you start with all that blood on your hands," Carly asked. "There is no rest for tortured souls, like you."

At that, the doctor looked at her and started to laugh. "God, you're such an innocent, so naïve. You're like some otherworldly child. No wonder Henry had no clue how to even deal with you. I should have seen it a long time ago. It would have given me the leverage I needed to make Henry leave you. Still, it worked out well in the end."

Declan asked, "This is your idea of it working out well? With everybody dead, so you don't have to worry about it, so your son is fine, and who gives a shit, is that it?"

"Somewhat, yes. Now move over to the other side of the counter," she told Declan. "I already ran lots of searches and checked you out, so I already know you're not capable of much of a fight. Which is probably why you got the damn dog. I guess if that's what Carly thinks she needs, whatever, though I would prefer a whole man myself."

Carly gasped. "I had no idea you were such a raving bitch."

"Yeah, I know. I try to be nice all the time, dealing with patients and all their *blah, blah, blah* bullshit problems. I'll tell you something. That wasn't much fun. I'm more than happy to be retired and to leave all that behind me."

"Good choice. At least now you cannot mess up anybody else's life with your lame advice," Carly added.

"Oh, don't go telling me how I messed yours up," Annie said, with an eye roll. "Anybody who would even talk to you back then would have helped you to some degree. God, you were pathetic. What a mess."

Carly felt the words slapping away at her self-confidence, but, as she stared at Annie, all she could see was a person consumed by hatred. She had allowed it to boil over until she had taken away everything that mattered. "You had no right to hurt them."

"Maybe not," Annie murmured. "What does it matter now? You won't do a damn thing about it." She laughed and fired a bullet into Declan's leg. As she fired, Declan lunged forward. Carly watched in horror as he grabbed Annie with both hands, his leg kicking her feet out from under her, and dropping her like a rock, flat on the ground. He landed on her, making her scream in pain.

"Oh, sorry. Did I hurt you?" Declan asked.

Such mockery was in his tone that Carly knew he didn't give a shit. She could hardly blame him. While he was having some revenge on Annie, Carly scooted over to check on Shelby. Thank God, it was just a graze. She was hardly bleeding and licked Carly's face, comforting her.

"Oh wait," Declan began, "I can't fight worth a damn either because you know, I have a prosthetic. I'm really not a man and all," he added, as he kicked the gun free. Looking over at Carly, he said, "Grab me some more of those zip ties, will you?"

In the distance, she heard sirens, but she raced to get the ties, and they quickly secured the doctor.

He looked over at Carly. "I was hoping the cops would get here soon."

"How did they even know?" she asked.

"Depends on how good of a job the EMTs did with Dean."

She stared at Declan and immediately pulled out her phone. Dean answered the phone, his voice raspy and rough. "Dean, are you okay?"

"Not at the moment, but they're working on me, and I'm on my way to the hospital. Are you okay?"

"Yes. We've got them here, both mother and son."

"Well, thank God for that." He hesitated, then said, "I've got to go."

"Which hospital?"

He quickly told her, and she said, "We'll meet you

there." With that, she hung up. She looked over at Declan. "We need to get you to the hospital too."

He looked at her, puzzled. "Why?"

"She shot you."

"No, she shot my prosthetic," he said, with a shrug. "She's not that good of a doctor. She shot the wrong leg. She thought she was taking out my good one." Then he shifted over to check on Shelby.

At that, Carly looked at him, then at Annie, who was spitting mad on the floor next to her still-whining son. Carly started to laugh.

When the police burst through the front door, the detective from before was near the front of the pack. Larry raced in and took one look. "Holy shit."

"Yeah, holy shit is right," Carly snapped. "You think you guys can mop this up? My father is headed to the hospital after this bitch shot him," she said, giving Annie a kick.

He frowned at her and asked, "Your *father*?"

She nodded. "Yeah, it turns out the other man, Dean, is my biological father. This guy here is the son of the man who raised me and is also the intruder who bashed me over the head, broke into my home, trashed my attic, and probably killed that squirrel. This conniving bitch is his mother, who murdered my parents, shot Declan, shot Shelby, and wanted to shoot me too. Confusing, I know." She did her best to give him the short version.

"We'll need to get formal statements from you, as soon as we get all this wrapped up," Larry stated.

"That's fine, but first I'll go to the hospital to see my real father."

And, with that, the dogs safely locked up, she dashed out with Declan. Carly wanted to drive, but Declan would have nothing to do with it. As soon as they pulled up to the hospital, she raced into the emergency department, only to find out her father was having surgery. She stared at the nurse. "How bad is it?"

"It's bad enough, given his age," she noted, "but he's pretty strong, and he's fighting hard. So all in all, I think he stands a good chance of getting through it."

"Thank you," Carly said. "That's very good news."

The two of them sat at the hospital for the next few hours, until her father came out of surgery. When the nurse finally came to them, she smiled and announced, "He's awake for the moment, but he won't be for long. So you have a few minutes to speak with him, if you hurry." She looked down at them and asked, "You are family, right?"

At that, Carly smiled and said, "Yes. He's my father."

The nurse nodded and motioned for them. "Follow me."

The nurse led her down to a room, holding Declan back at the door.

"Go ahead," Declan told Carly.

"It can only be family right now," the nurse stated.

"He's my fiancé," Carly said immediately, "and I know my father would want to see him."

The nurse hesitated, then nodded. "Go ahead, but only for a few minutes. I can't have you upsetting him."

"Believe me. That's not my intention." When she stepped into the room, Dean turned his head to look at her and smiled.

"Hey, you made it."

"Did you call the cops for us?" she asked.

He nodded. "I wondered if that's where she was heading. Oh my God, that woman."

"I know, but now she's in custody, and her son is too."

He nodded. "But not before she shot me."

"But, because they shot you and a few other people and dogs and things," Declan added at her side, "they'll go to jail for a very long time. She's also the one who murdered Carly's parents."

At that, Dean nodded slowly. "She took great delight in explaining it all to me, right before she shot me, and the fact that her son was actually Henry's child."

Carly nodded. "I can't even imagine what all went on in their marriage. I always thought they were happy. Reserved but happy."

"I did too," Dean noted. "Otherwise I would have persuaded her to leave him. Honestly I did try at first, but I thought she had only spent time with me to get back at Henry because she was so hurt. But to discover that he didn't even care? I just wish …" Dean stared morosely at the ceiling above him.

"At least we know the truth now," Declan said. "Henry manufactured the evidence against you."

Dean winced. "I figured that out in jail. I had plenty of time to think about it all, and when nothing else makes any sense, and you're left with one thing, that one thing tends to be the truth. I just didn't know how to get any proof. I didn't want to suffer any longer, and I sure as hell didn't want my legacy to be one of failure and deceit."

"Well, I'm sure we can work to get your name cleared, and hopefully some restitution for all the years that you were put away," Declan added, his arms wrapped around Carly's shoulders. He pulled her close and said, "Now Carly can get some peace, knowing that chapter of her life is over."

"Not only is that one over," Carly replied, "another chapter is beginning." She stepped next to the bed to pick up

Dean's hand. "That new chapter has room for you as well—if you want to have anything to do with me, that is."

He stared at her in shock, tears filling his eyes. "My dear, I have wanted nothing more than that ever since I found out. It always was in the back of my mind, but, without any way to know for sure, the possibility tormented me endlessly."

"I think Mom will be happy too."

"She never answered me after the first time I asked because that was her way. She considered the discussion closed, and that was that." Still he smiled. "I really did love her though."

"So did I," Carly said, "and I loved Henry. Obviously both of them had some character issues I wasn't aware of and would have preferred not knowing about, but I'll just have to come to terms with it and move on."

"I'm sorry about Annie," Dean muttered. "When I realized that was who you'd been to see, it reminded me of the relationship she had had way back when, and I realized that she quite possibly was Henry's affair."

"And even then you intimated as much to me."

"Yes, but I didn't think you knew anything about it, and I didn't want to stir up more problems. At some point, years ago, Annie contacted me. She actually came to visit me in prison. I told her what my intentions were, whenever I got out. That, I can only assume, is what started it all up. If I had been content to stay a guilty party for the rest of my life and to never be a cleared man, it might never have happened. Your parents might have been alive too."

"No, that's not so," Carly disagreed. "Seeing you that day convinced Annie that you were my biological father. The resemblance had grown stronger as I got older. That hate had been festering inside Annie for far too long. She'd been planning to kill my mother all these years anyway but had held off, believing Henry's promises. His refusal to continue paying her blackmail demands set her off, and the fact that he'd stayed with my mother all those years because of me made it all the more ironic, once Annie knew the truth. They argued, and she took great delight in telling him the truth, that *you* were my father. Then at some point, Annie confronted my mother as well. Then things all got out of hand, and Annie shot them both and walked away."

Dean winced at that. "I'm so sorry."

"Yeah, me too, but I do have to find a way to move on, and one of the ways I'd like to do that is by having you in my life. I think we've lost enough time, haven't we?" He gave her a beautiful smile, tremulous and shaky, but still a wondrous smile.

She leaned over and kissed him on the cheek and whispered, "Now, you need to get some rest and heal." And, with that, she took a step back.

He gave her a two-finger wave and said, "As long as I get to see you when I wake up, I'll make sure that I do."

"I hope so. I feel like I've done without family for a long time. Even back when I had both my parents, I was a fish out of water. We'll have to see if I'm more like you." Carly laughed. "I think my mother always knew. I think it was always in the back of her mind because, every once in a while, I would do something, and she'd give me the oddest look, as if it were something she expected from somebody else."

"I wouldn't be at all surprised. My family has always thrown strong genetics, but, with the love of my life already tied up with somebody else, I never did find another person I cared about in the same way."

With that and Declan's arm still around her shoulders, Carly nodded.

Her father's eyelids shut, but then flew open again. "I'm still here," he said, his voice a little stronger. He looked at Declan. "Seeing as I am now officially her father, I'd like to know what your intentions are, young man."

Declan laughed. "Well, you know what? That's kind of funny because, when we were trying to come in here, your daughter looked that nurse right in the eye and said I was her fiancé, since only relatives are allowed in. So, I'm thinking that I'd better have her back on that and let her make an honest man out of me."

She gasped, then turned to look at him, her face alight with laughter. "Oh, that would be too funny."

"Actually," Dean said, "considering what I've seen of the two of you, I think it's one hell of an idea."

She looked at him, then looked back at Declan. "Seriously?"

"Yeah," Declan confirmed. "I mean, it's not as if you asked me though." She just stared at him, her jaw dropped. He chuckled, pulling her closer. "I won't put you on the spot like that. I mean, if that's not where your heart lies and you were just toying with my affections," he teased, his hand resting on his heart, as if torn by her actions.

Smiling, she shook her head. "Oh, you." Turning to Dean, her father beamed with parental pride. "Besides, we can't possibly get married while you're in the hospital."

His eyes widened. "I'll get out real soon." Then he stopped and asked, "Are you asking me to walk you down the aisle?"

There was such hope in his heart and joy on his face that she leaned over, kissed him again, and said, "Absolutely. You are my father after all," she stated, with a bright smile. "Now I'm taking this very mischievous man out of here before he causes all of us to have a heart attack." She chuckled. "And you need to get some sleep." And, with that she turned and pushed Declan ahead of her into the hallway.

As soon as they got outside of Dean's room, Declan wrapped her up, spun her around, and pulled her into his arms. "Did you mean it?"

"Did I mean what?" she asked, her eyes sparkling. "I should be asking if *you* meant it."

"Well, how about we just take all the guesswork out of it then, and I'll just ask the question."

Her eyes widened. "We don't have to do anything about it right here and now," she said hurriedly. "We have time."

"Not if you don't want to." However he grabbed her chin and closed her mouth. "Now, you get to open it for one thing and one thing only," he said, his voice a deep sexy whisper. "Carly Simpson, will you marry me, please?"

She looked up at him. "Why would you want to marry me?" she asked, her voice as husky as his.

He smiled and whispered, "Because I love you. Because somehow, … when I saw you that first day, my heart soared, and I knew it had to be love. I've been trying to go slow, to give you time, and to let you see that we'll be really good together. But now that I know you're safe, I'm really not sure I can wait much longer."

"We hardly know each other."

"Well, we'll just have to spend the rest of our engagement taking care of that," he stated, with a thick voice. "But I really need to know if you have any of these same feelings that I have."

She looped her arms around his neck, leaning forward

until their foreheads were touching. "I absolutely feel the same way," she murmured. "Ever since you walked into my life, it's been complete chaos, but there's been one solid center in that storm, and that has been you."

"So, does that mean the answer is yes?"

"It does. So do you think we can go home now and maybe, you know, try out my bed?"

His eyes widened. "Oh, good God, can we?"

She burst out laughing and looked over to see the nurse standing there, with a beaming grin on her face.

"I sure hope I heard what I just heard," she shared, "because I'm a sucker for happy endings. Now, would you two go home and let me look after your father?"

And, with that, Declan grabbed Carly's hand, and they raced out of the hospital.

As soon as they got home, Declan headed through the kitchen and opened up the door for the dogs.

"How is Shelby doing?" Carly asked.

"She's good. It's just a scratch. We'll need to keep it wrapped for a few days to keep it clean, but that's it." He checked it over, and Shelby was soaking up the attention. "She'll need lots of extra cuddles for a while."

"She can have all the love and cuddles she could possibly soak up," Carly replied, bending down to hug her.

"You might need a bigger bedroom," Declan suggested. "With all these dogs, no way they'll want to sleep anywhere but with us."

"I don't blame them, but you're right. If nothing else, we might need to get them their own bed."

"Speaking of beds," he said, waggling his eyebrows.

She grinned, darted past him, pulling her T-shirt over her head, as she dropped it off to the side, even as she unclipped her bra and threw it down the stairs. "Ha, I can run faster than you!" When she got to the bed, she was tripping to get out of her shoes, socks, and jeans, but, by the time she fell onto the bed, completely nude and laughing hysterically, she looked up to see him already standing there and stripped naked as well. Then she saw the prosthetic.

Her laughter died as she got up, walked over, and her finger swirled along the top of the cotton padding.

"Is it that bad?" he asked, his voice soft.

"Not at all. The question is, how bad was it for you?" she asked, not realizing tears were in her eyes. "I hate to think of you hurt like this and that you went through it all alone. Being alone sucks."

"It does." He pulled her up, wrapping his arms around her. "But guess what?"

She looked at him, one eyebrow lifted. "What?"

"Neither of us is alone anymore, and we never have to feel that way again."

She reached her arms around his waist and snuggled against his strong chest. "Thank God for that. I can't believe you just breezed into my life, made yourself at home, and here we are."

"Well, if I hadn't, we would both still be alone." He leaned over, kissed her thoroughly, then picked her up and dropped her on the big springy mattress.

With a shriek of laughter, she bounced and then opened her arms to him. "You better get your ass down here."

And, with a grin, he looked at his leg and asked, "On or off?"

"Oh, definitely on. Nothing like a man of steel." Her eyebrows waggled and, with a laugh, she asked, "Now for the question of the hour. Is all of you made of steel?"

Loving her repartee, he grinned. "We'll just have to find out, won't we?" And, with that, he came down on the bed beside her, pulled her into his arms. "Thank God, I found you. Sometimes I wondered if I'd ever find anybody."

"I know what you mean. I felt that way too, and it sucks. But …" She planted little kisses across his chin, his cheeks, and down his neck, before running her fingers through his soft wavy hair. "We have each other, and that's what we need to hold on to."

He lowered his head, and he kissed her, starting a firestorm that swept through them both. By the time he lifted his head, he was panting, and her eyes were almost crossed. "Dear God, I just want more and more." And he lowered his head again. This time there was no time, there was no patience. It was like a fury of energy coming together in a maelstrom, and, by the time he entered her body, she was already shuddering in his arms over and over again.

She finally lay here quietly, staring up at him in wonder. "Oh my God, you *are* a man of steel."

He burst out laughing, as he collapsed beside her, pulling her into his arms. "Only for you, my dear, only for you."

She closed her eyes and snuggled in close.

Just then came a bark from the doorway. Declan looked over to see Shelby. He snorted and said, "Come on, girl."

She jumped up onto the bed from a standing leap, making the bed bounce, and, with that invitation, and a little help, came all the rest of the dogs. Laughing and giggling, they reached out to love the rest of their family.

Carly asked him, "So, will you work with Shelby? Man, I

don't know what kind of training you were doing, but it was certainly effective."

"That's what I was thinking. I do have an income, you know. It goes along with this whole medical thing, so I was thinking of maybe doing search and rescue and some K9 work. I'm not too sure of the details yet. Plus I'm still trying to figure out what all Shelby can do."

"How about other dogs like her?"

"I'm not against that," he said, "and you do have the room." Then he stopped, looked down at her, and asked, "If it's okay if I move in?"

"Hell yes," she said, "and, if this doesn't suit, we can sell it and buy something else."

He nodded. "That's a possibility too. I do have money, so we can figure out what we want together. But, at least for now, until we figure it all out, I kind of like this place. With a few renos, and an extension out back, I think it'll work perfect for our extended family."

She frowned. "Extended family?"

He nodded. "The little pattering of feet, plus lots of furry paws."

She beamed. "You know something? That sounds perfect. I always hated being an only child."

"So did I. So, I suggest we fill this house with lots and lots of laughter." She wrapped her arms around him, and he closed his eyes. "I'm so damn grateful for Badger and Kat for sending me here."

"Me too," she whispered hugging him close.

Now Declan just had to remember to thank them for it later.

EPILOGUE

Kat stared at Badger. "There's such a miraculous note to these endings," she whispered.

Badger nodded, his voice equally soft as he spoke, after the phone call ended. "Who would have thought that Declan would have wrapped that up so nicely. Not only a cold case on her family's murder but the attacks against Carly leading up to this, and he secured the War Dog."

Kat shook her head. "I know it's a twisted world out there, but, dear God, that's quite a story."

"And yet here we are, doing our part to actually fix things."

"Declan wants to keep Shelby then?"

"Oh, I think it's probably the best answer in this case, as they get to share the dog." Badger smiled. "Shelby might do well with the hospitals too, but she will definitely do well in terms of various K9 work."

"That's huge, absolutely huge. My God." Kat gave a big sigh and placed her hand on her chest. "My heart actually swells, I'm so happy."

He smiled at her. "That's because you're such a good person."

She chuckled. "Well, this has been one hell of an experience. I know we're not making any money on it, and money isn't the point, but, wow, are we ever affecting lives."

"In a good way." Badger nodded. "It's all very hard to imagine." Then he looked down at the file in front of him. "It makes we wish we could help others, even if not through this K9 program."

"You're thinking of Timber, aren't you?" Kat smiled at her husband. "He's doing very well."

"I know he is. That man seems to be able to do anything when it comes to construction work. I did ask him if he found out more about that property he was interested in, and he said, yes. And that was it. No update. No further response." Badger laughed. "I can't even consider him unfriendly, as he answered me with a smile."

"Well, there you go. When he's ready to share, he will."

"We'll miss him, if he decides to do something other than help us."

"Maybe we should consider a construction side to our current businesses."

Badger snorted. "Like we don't have one now. Although, if Timber wanted to do something along that line, I'd support him. He really knows what he's doing."

"So maybe bring it up with him. I know he's fighting his own demons, but it never hurts to remind someone that they aren't alone." She smiled at Badger, watching as he fingered the file in front of him. "You've got another one, don't you?"

He nodded. "I do. I was wondering about Bauer."

"Not Timber? Bauer, *huh*? Wasn't he setting up a search and rescue operation around here?"

"He was thinking about it, but something holds him back. He just keeps talking about it. I've asked him to take one of these jobs over and over again, but he keeps saying no, tells me that he's not ready."

"Any reason why not?"

"Because he had a K9 dog, who saved Bauer's life, but he lost the dog. Of course Bauer lost a leg and a hand in the deal, so overall, it left him with a bad taste for the military."

"Right, we're still working to get that one prosthetic right, but otherwise he's been doing really well."

Badger nodded. "I'd like to see him do one of these jobs and get him over the hump and to see if that kind of work is really what he wants."

"It's funny because I do remember you talking to him about this last year."

Badger smiled. "Yeah, because I know that's where his heart is, and I wanted to see if he could get past being stuck and actually help one of these animals."

"Does he know it's something that he needs to get through?"

"I don't know. I've talked to him a bunch of times, but—"

"Where's the dog?"

"Well, that's another reason for it. Otherwise I'd be tempted to do it myself."

Kat looked at her husband in surprise. "Do you want a War Dog? I mean, I'm sure one of these dogs could become yours if you wanted one."

"I don't know," Badger admitted. "I've been thinking about it. I mean, you hear these stories, and you wonder."

"Oh, wait, hang on a minute. I get it. You're looking for a new woman, aren't you?"

He grinned at her. "Oh, dang, busted. Come on. Do you think you aren't more than enough woman for me? Not to mention the *kids*," he added, with an eye roll.

"Absolutely. So, come on. Tell me about this one. Then let's give Bauer a call."

"Well, that's the thing. This War Dog is a big male, missing a back leg. It was adopted, then he had more medical problems, and that's when they took off the leg. Then they abandoned it at the vet clinic."

"Seriously?"

He nodded.

Kat frowned. "And it's local, right? So this really isn't a search and rescue or a hunt-and-retrieve type thing."

"Not really, no, but I talked to the vet about it, and you do know the vet."

"Sure, if we're talking about Mags."

"We are, indeed, talking about Mags," Badger confirmed, "and I know she's a good friend of yours, but, hey, she is single."

At that, Kat stared at him in surprise. "You're not actively matchmaking, are you?"

"No, of course not," he declared immediately.

She rolled her eyes. "Of course you are. How else do you explain all these happy-ending K9 cases?"

"Well, they weren't solely about matchmaking," he replied in a dry tone. "I know Bauer wants to stay local with his new job, but I thought maybe he might want to work with this dog some."

"But why did it end up in our files, if it's local and if it's already here?"

"Because, in this case, the dog doesn't have a home."

"So we're supposed to do an adoption for it? That's hardly within the scope of how we started."

"Well, as you know, everything here that we started has kind of changed over time, but it's also because Mags phoned me this morning."

She looked at him in surprise. "When?"

"Yeah, I would have told you about it, but Declan called when you walked in, so I haven't had a chance."

"What's the matter?"

"His name's Toby, the War Dog, I mean. Mags had a stranger come into her place yesterday, who took a real shine to the dog, and she told the guy that all the adoption information had to go through us. He apparently got really ugly about it. So, when she came in this morning, there had been a break-in, and the dog is missing."

"Ah, shit."

"So now she feels guilty as hell, and Toby is missing."

Kat stared at him. "And you're thinking Bauer is the guy for the job?"

"Well, Bauer knows the area. Bauer knows dogs. Bauer knows Mags." Then he shot Kat a sideways look.

She stared at him for a long moment. "You know what? It just might work. Mags is pretty definite about not getting involved again though. She says she only wants to be around animals."

"Which is also Bauer's point. He isn't in any hurry to get involved with anyone again, not after his wife walked away with his best friend while he was overseas."

Kat winced at that. "Right, I had heard that. Mags is a veterinarian with a kind heart who looks after animals. Then there's Bauer, who is a little bit on the rough side, yet—you know something?" Kat looked at Badger in surprise. "You're getting pretty good at this."

"Well, Bauer hasn't said yes though."

At that came a laugh at the doorway, and they both looked up to see Bauer, leaning against the door.

"What are you two hatching now?" he asked in disgust. "It better not have anything to do with my love life."

"No, not at all," Badger replied. "Do you know the vet here, Mags?"

He straightened. "Sure, why?"

"Her clinic got broken into this morning."

At that news, Bauer straightened and glared at Badger. "What?"

"Yeah, and the War Dog that I mentioned to you is now missing." Badger then explained what Mags had told him on the phone this morning.

"Well, that little punk bastard isn't taking a dog that's already struggling and go out and do what with Toby? If that's how this punk treats the vet, you know he'll treat the dog like shit."

"I know, and you know what will end up happening with a guy like that."

"Yeah, the dog'll go after him, after it's taken all it can handle."

"So, Mags really needs a hand," Badger said, looking at him. "She feels terrible."

Bauer glared. "I'm heading to the vet clinic right now." He spun back to the doorway.

"So, does that mean you're taking the case?" Badger asked.

Bauer turned and asked, "What do you mean *case*?"

"Remember? I talked to you about all these War Dogs?"

"Sure, but I wouldn't do it." Then he frowned and asked, "Is that what this is?"

Badger nodded. "It is. Mags was just checking the dog over because it was abandoned. Someone had brought it to her. When she scanned it, she realized it was a War Dog and contacted us."

"Well hell," Bauer muttered. "Looks like you'll get your

way then."

"And what does that mean? I really need you to be clear about this," Badger said.

Bauer glared at him and saw the grin on Badger's face. "Hell yes, you know I won't let a loser punk steal a War Dog like that. Besides, Mags is one hell of a vet. If she needs a hand, I'll be there." And, with that, he stormed off.

Kat looked over at her husband and smiled. "That was dirty."

"Hey, it worked, didn't it?" Badger noted, with a smile. "Now we just have to let nature take its course."

This concludes Book 21 of The K9 Files: Declan.
Read about Bauer: The K9 Files, Book 22

The K9 Files: Bauer (Book #22)

Welcome to the all new K9 Files series reconnecting readers with the unforgettable men from SEALs of Steel in a new series of action packed, page turning romantic suspense that fans have come to expect from USA TODAY Bestselling author Dale Mayer. Pssst... you'll meet other favorite characters from SEALs of Honor and Heroes for Hire too!

Staying in town suited Bauer. Dealing with Kat and Badger's matchingmaking? Not so much. But, when a mutual friend calls to say an injured War Dog was dropped off at her clinic—only to then be stolen during the night after she completed surgery to fix his injured stump—well, Bauer is all over it.

Mags always liked Bauer, but she kept her personal relationships short and sweet. After all, commitments were too often broken and the resultant pain horrific. However, Bauer refuses to leave her in trouble and is here for her every step of the way; plus they share the love of animals. How can she ignore all that? Plus he is a hell of a package. But is she willing to take a chance on being hurt again?

The escalating danger—surrounding Toby, her injured War Dog—catches Mags and Bauer in a web of risk that can only end one way ...

Find Book 22 here!
To find out more visit Dale Mayer's website.
https://geni.us/DMSBauer

Author's Note

Thank you for reading Declan: The K9 Files, Book 21! If you enjoyed the book, please take a moment and leave a short review.

Dear reader,

I love to hear from readers, and you can contact me at my website: www.dalemayer.com or at my Facebook author page. To be informed of new releases and special offers, sign up for my newsletter or follow me on BookBub. And if you are interested in joining Dale Mayer's Reader Group, here is the Facebook sign up page.
http://geni.us/DaleMayerFBGroup

Cheers,
Dale Mayer

About the Author

Dale Mayer is a *USA Today* best-selling author, best known for her SEALs military romances, her Psychic Visions series, and her Lovely Lethal Garden cozy series. Her contemporary romances are raw and full of passion and emotion (Broken But … Mending, Hathaway House series). Her thrillers will keep you guessing (Kate Morgan, By Death series), and her romantic comedies will keep you giggling (*It's a Dog's Life*, a stand-alone novella; and the Broken Protocols series, starring Charming Marvin, the cat).

Dale honors the stories that come to her—and some of them are crazy, break all the rules and cross multiple genres!

To go with her fiction, she also writes nonfiction in many different fields, with books available on résumé writing, companion gardening, and the US mortgage system. All her books are available in print and ebook format.

Connect with Dale Mayer Online

Dale's Website – www.dalemayer.com
Twitter – @DaleMayer
Facebook Page – geni.us/DaleMayerFBFanPage
Facebook Group – geni.us/DaleMayerFBGroup
BookBub – geni.us/DaleMayerBookbub
Instagram – geni.us/DaleMayerInstagram
Goodreads – geni.us/DaleMayerGoodreads
Newsletter – geni.us/DaleNews

Also by Dale Mayer

Published Adult Books:

Shadow Recon
Magnus, Book 1
Rogan, Book 2
Egan, Book 3
Barret, Book 4
Whalen, Book 5
Nikolai, Book 6

Bullard's Battle
Ryland's Reach, Book 1
Cain's Cross, Book 2
Eton's Escape, Book 3
Garret's Gambit, Book 4
Kano's Keep, Book 5
Fallon's Flaw, Book 6
Quinn's Quest, Book 7
Bullard's Beauty, Book 8
Bullard's Best, Book 9
Bullard's Battle, Books 1–2
Bullard's Battle, Books 3–4
Bullard's Battle, Books 5–6
Bullard's Battle, Books 7–8

Terkel's Team
Damon's Deal, Book 1
Wade's War, Book 2
Gage's Goal, Book 3
Calum's Contact, Book 4
Rick's Road, Book 5
Scott's Summit, Book 6
Brody's Beast, Book 7
Terkel's Twist, Book 8
Terkel's Triumph, Book 9

Terk's Guardians
Radar, Book 1
Legend, Book 2

Kate Morgan
Simon Says… Hide, Book 1
Simon Says… Jump, Book 2
Simon Says… Ride, Book 3
Simon Says… Scream, Book 4
Simon Says… Run, Book 5
Simon Says… Walk, Book 6
Simon Says… Forgive, Book 7

Hathaway House
Aaron, Book 1
Brock, Book 2
Cole, Book 3
Denton, Book 4
Elliot, Book 5
Finn, Book 6
Gregory, Book 7

Heath, Book 8
Iain, Book 9
Jaden, Book 10
Keith, Book 11
Lance, Book 12
Melissa, Book 13
Nash, Book 14
Owen, Book 15
Percy, Book 16
Quinton, Book 17
Ryatt, Book 18
Spencer, Book 19
Timothy, Book 20
Urban, Book 21
Hathaway House, Books 1–3
Hathaway House, Books 4–6
Hathaway House, Books 7–9

The K9 Files
Ethan, Book 1
Pierce, Book 2
Zane, Book 3
Blaze, Book 4
Lucas, Book 5
Parker, Book 6
Carter, Book 7
Weston, Book 8
Greyson, Book 9
Rowan, Book 10
Caleb, Book 11
Kurt, Book 12
Tucker, Book 13

Harley, Book 14
Kyron, Book 15
Jenner, Book 16
Rhys, Book 17
Landon, Book 18
Harper, Book 19
Kascius, Book 20
Declan, Book 21
Bauer, Book 22
The K9 Files, Books 1–2
The K9 Files, Books 3–4
The K9 Files, Books 5–6
The K9 Files, Books 7–8
The K9 Files, Books 9–10
The K9 Files, Books 11–12

Lovely Lethal Gardens
Arsenic in the Azaleas, Book 1
Bones in the Begonias, Book 2
Corpse in the Carnations, Book 3
Daggers in the Dahlias, Book 4
Evidence in the Echinacea, Book 5
Footprints in the Ferns, Book 6
Gun in the Gardenias, Book 7
Handcuffs in the Heather, Book 8
Ice Pick in the Ivy, Book 9
Jewels in the Juniper, Book 10
Killer in the Kiwis, Book 11
Lifeless in the Lilies, Book 12
Murder in the Marigolds, Book 13
Nabbed in the Nasturtiums, Book 14
Offed in the Orchids, Book 15

Poison in the Pansies, Book 16
Quarry in the Quince, Book 17
Revenge in the Roses, Book 18
Silenced in the Sunflowers, Book 19
Toes up in the Tulips, Book 20
Uzi in the Urn, Book 21
Victim in the Violets, Book 22
Lovely Lethal Gardens, Books 1–2
Lovely Lethal Gardens, Books 3–4
Lovely Lethal Gardens, Books 5–6
Lovely Lethal Gardens, Books 7–8
Lovely Lethal Gardens, Books 9–10

Psychic Visions Series
Tuesday's Child
Hide 'n Go Seek
Maddy's Floor
Garden of Sorrow
Knock Knock…
Rare Find
Eyes to the Soul
Now You See Her
Shattered
Into the Abyss
Seeds of Malice
Eye of the Falcon
Itsy-Bitsy Spider
Unmasked
Deep Beneath
From the Ashes
Stroke of Death
Ice Maiden

Snap, Crackle…
What If…
Talking Bones
String of Tears
Inked Forever
Insanity
Psychic Visions Books 1–3
Psychic Visions Books 4–6
Psychic Visions Books 7–9

By Death Series
Touched by Death
Haunted by Death
Chilled by Death
By Death Books 1–3

Broken Protocols – Romantic Comedy Series
Cat's Meow
Cat's Pajamas
Cat's Cradle
Cat's Claus
Broken Protocols 1-4

Broken and… Mending
Skin
Scars
Scales (of Justice)
Broken but… Mending 1-3

Glory
Genesis
Tori
Celeste

Glory Trilogy

Biker Blues
Morgan: Biker Blues, Volume 1
Cash: Biker Blues, Volume 2

SEALs of Honor
Mason: SEALs of Honor, Book 1
Hawk: SEALs of Honor, Book 2
Dane: SEALs of Honor, Book 3
Swede: SEALs of Honor, Book 4
Shadow: SEALs of Honor, Book 5
Cooper: SEALs of Honor, Book 6
Markus: SEALs of Honor, Book 7
Evan: SEALs of Honor, Book 8
Mason's Wish: SEALs of Honor, Book 9
Chase: SEALs of Honor, Book 10
Brett: SEALs of Honor, Book 11
Devlin: SEALs of Honor, Book 12
Easton: SEALs of Honor, Book 13
Ryder: SEALs of Honor, Book 14
Macklin: SEALs of Honor, Book 15
Corey: SEALs of Honor, Book 16
Warrick: SEALs of Honor, Book 17
Tanner: SEALs of Honor, Book 18
Jackson: SEALs of Honor, Book 19
Kanen: SEALs of Honor, Book 20
Nelson: SEALs of Honor, Book 21
Taylor: SEALs of Honor, Book 22
Colton: SEALs of Honor, Book 23
Troy: SEALs of Honor, Book 24
Axel: SEALs of Honor, Book 25

Baylor: SEALs of Honor, Book 26
Hudson: SEALs of Honor, Book 27
Lachlan: SEALs of Honor, Book 28
Paxton: SEALs of Honor, Book 29
Bronson: SEALs of Honor, Book 30
Hale: SEALs of Honor, Book 31
SEALs of Honor, Books 1–3
SEALs of Honor, Books 4–6
SEALs of Honor, Books 7–10
SEALs of Honor, Books 11–13
SEALs of Honor, Books 14–16
SEALs of Honor, Books 17–19
SEALs of Honor, Books 20–22
SEALs of Honor, Books 23–25

Heroes for Hire
Levi's Legend: Heroes for Hire, Book 1
Stone's Surrender: Heroes for Hire, Book 2
Merk's Mistake: Heroes for Hire, Book 3
Rhodes's Reward: Heroes for Hire, Book 4
Flynn's Firecracker: Heroes for Hire, Book 5
Logan's Light: Heroes for Hire, Book 6
Harrison's Heart: Heroes for Hire, Book 7
Saul's Sweetheart: Heroes for Hire, Book 8
Dakota's Delight: Heroes for Hire, Book 9
Tyson's Treasure: Heroes for Hire, Book 10
Jace's Jewel: Heroes for Hire, Book 11
Rory's Rose: Heroes for Hire, Book 12
Brandon's Bliss: Heroes for Hire, Book 13
Liam's Lily: Heroes for Hire, Book 14
North's Nikki: Heroes for Hire, Book 15
Anders's Angel: Heroes for Hire, Book 16

Reyes's Raina: Heroes for Hire, Book 17
Dezi's Diamond: Heroes for Hire, Book 18
Vince's Vixen: Heroes for Hire, Book 19
Ice's Icing: Heroes for Hire, Book 20
Johan's Joy: Heroes for Hire, Book 21
Galen's Gemma: Heroes for Hire, Book 22
Zack's Zest: Heroes for Hire, Book 23
Bonaparte's Belle: Heroes for Hire, Book 24
Noah's Nemesis: Heroes for Hire, Book 25
Tomas's Trials: Heroes for Hire, Book 26
Carson's Choice: Heroes for Hire, Book 27
Dante's Decision: Heroes for Hire, Book 28
Steven's Solace: Heroes for Hire, Book 29
Heroes for Hire, Books 1–3
Heroes for Hire, Books 4–6
Heroes for Hire, Books 7–9
Heroes for Hire, Books 10–12
Heroes for Hire, Books 13–15
Heroes for Hire, Books 16–18
Heroes for Hire, Books 19–21
Heroes for Hire, Books 22–24

SEALs of Steel

Badger: SEALs of Steel, Book 1
Erick: SEALs of Steel, Book 2
Cade: SEALs of Steel, Book 3
Talon: SEALs of Steel, Book 4
Laszlo: SEALs of Steel, Book 5
Geir: SEALs of Steel, Book 6
Jager: SEALs of Steel, Book 7
The Final Reveal: SEALs of Steel, Book 8
SEALs of Steel, Books 1–4

SEALs of Steel, Books 5–8
SEALs of Steel, Books 1–8

The Mavericks
Kerrick, Book 1
Griffin, Book 2
Jax, Book 3
Beau, Book 4
Asher, Book 5
Ryker, Book 6
Miles, Book 7
Nico, Book 8
Keane, Book 9
Lennox, Book 10
Gavin, Book 11
Shane, Book 12
Diesel, Book 13
Jerricho, Book 14
Killian, Book 15
Hatch, Book 16
Corbin, Book 17
Aiden, Book 18
The Mavericks, Books 1–2
The Mavericks, Books 3–4
The Mavericks, Books 5–6
The Mavericks, Books 7–8
The Mavericks, Books 9–10
The Mavericks, Books 11–12

Standalone Novellas
It's a Dog's Life
Riana's Revenge

Second Chances

Published Young Adult Books:

Family Blood Ties Series
Vampire in Denial
Vampire in Distress
Vampire in Design
Vampire in Deceit
Vampire in Defiance
Vampire in Conflict
Vampire in Chaos
Vampire in Crisis
Vampire in Control
Vampire in Charge
Family Blood Ties Set 1–3
Family Blood Ties Set 1–5
Family Blood Ties Set 4–6
Family Blood Ties Set 7–9
Sian's Solution, A Family Blood Ties Series Prequel Novelette

Design series
Dangerous Designs
Deadly Designs
Darkest Designs
Design Series Trilogy

Standalone
In Cassie's Corner
Gem Stone (a Gemma Stone Mystery)
Time Thieves

Published Non-Fiction Books:

Career Essentials
Career Essentials: The Résumé
Career Essentials: The Cover Letter
Career Essentials: The Interview
Career Essentials: 3 in 1

Made in the USA
Columbia, SC
23 October 2023